Can AI Be Humorous?

Can AI Be Humorous?

Exploring the Lighter Side of AI
—Laugh and Learn

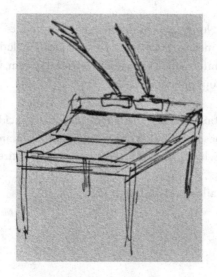

Writing before AI

Tom G. Anderson

Library of Congress Control Number: 2024916045
ISBN: Softcover   979-8-3694-2694-4
                 eBook   979-8-3694-2695-1

Print information available on the last page.

Rev. date: 08/21/2024

To order additional copies of this book, contact:
Xlibris
844-714-8691
www.Xlibris.com
Orders@Xlibris.com
861304

Contents

Acknowledgments

I was inspired and excited by a quick demo of ChatGPT by Mark Nielsen. He enthusiastically showed me how amazing it was and how ultra-fast it produced impressive results. He also showed me it could write like a 6th grade student or a college professor. How could I resist not writing a book using ChatGPT3.5 after seeing a stimulating demo? Also, a friend created a self-published book using AI and this served as an inspiration and model and showed me it could actually be done. Also, I'd like to pass on genuine thanks to Carl Anderson and Nancy Anderson who reviewed the book and offered suggestions for improvement and for Ed Perry for the idea to add the O. Henry vignette. In addition, Erika Nielsen contributed ideas related to the real life experience of raising two active children.

Dedication

This book is dedicated to my wonderful wife Nancy and to Dr. Shane Dormady, my medical oncologist and to Dr. Robert Sinha, my radiation oncologist, who have driven my Stage IV metastatic cancer into "complete remission".

Introduction

Humor is something I truly enjoy. I love cartoons and enjoy humorous language. The more surprising and exaggerated the cartoons and humor, the better I like it. Having spent a career in Silicon Valley, new technologies have always interested me. When AI came along with its powerful, once in a generation functionality, potential, and power, I wanted to learn about it so I thought I would start with ChatGPT 3.5. Why ChatGPT 3.5? It's widely known and free thus encouraging more people to try it and experience AI for themselves. Experience has taught me the fastest way to learn a new technology is to quickly become a user and experience it first-hand.

So I thought to myself why not marry humor and AI and the result is this book.

At first, when I started writing this book, I did not show the input to chat, just the output. I thought a series of stories written by chat would be great. However, nearly everyone I talked to about writing a book using AI immediately wanted to know, "How much did I write vs. how much did ChatGPT write?" This seemed to be a universal question, so I have a few original vignettes that do not show the input, but most use the current format: (1) My input, (2) ChatGPT output, and (3) my comments. The last section "What I Learned from Using AI" should not be skipped as it is an essential summary of the strengths and weaknesses of ChatGPT.

By the way, and this is a critical point, I am in no way an expert in ChatGPT and don't claim to be. I am an amateur who is just a user of ChatGPT. You can think of me as an explorer fascinated with this new incredibly powerful tool. Join me on this new adventure-laugh and learn!

Just a quick note, for convenience's sake, "ChatGPT" will at times be shortened to just "chat".

MY INPUT: **The dermatologist**

Write a humorous definition of a dermatologist. Name the doctor Dr. Constant Itch.

ChatGPT output:

Dr. Constant Itch: A dermatologist, known affectionately as the "skin whisperer" or the "itch detective," is a medical magician who specializes in deciphering the cryptic language of our body's largest organ - the skin. Armed with magnifying glasses and an arsenal of creams, Dr. Constant Itch fearlessly battles the nefarious foes of eczema, acne, and mysterious rashes. Their superpower? They can make you laugh while prescribing an ointment for that embarrassing rash in a place you'd rather not discuss at the dinner table. So, if you're ever feeling like your skin is staging a rebellion, fear not! Dr. Constant Itch is here to scratch that itch, both figuratively and literally!

My comments:

Excellent humor, especially the part about the dinner table.

MY INPUT: **The ophthalmologist**

Write a humorous definition of an ophthalmologist. Name the doctor Dr. Seymore Spots.

ChatGPT output:

Dr. Seymore Spots: The illustrious ophthalmologist, affectionately known as "the eye guy" or "the vision virtuoso," is the wizard of the ocular realm. Armed with a formidable array of lenses and gadgets that look like they belong in a sci-fi movie, Dr. Seymore Spots fearlessly delves into the mysterious depths of the eyeball. Their mission? To decipher the enigmatic hieroglyphics of the retina, cornea, and all things optic. With a flick of the wrist and a "please look into the light," they can diagnose conditions faster than you can say "20/20 vision." So, if you're seeing spots, feeling cross-eyed, or just need someone to tell you that yes, your eyes are indeed bloodshot from binge-watching Netflix, fear not! Dr. Seymore Spots is on the case, ready to bring clarity to even the most perplexing of peepers!

My comments:

Wonderful humor. I loved the "binge-watching Netflix" phrase.

MY INPUT: The podiatrist

Write a humorous definition of a podiatrist. Name the doctor Dr. Stubya Toe.

ChatGPT output:

Dr. Stubya Toe: Ah, the podiatrist, the unsung hero of the foot world! Dr. Stubya Toe, also known as the "sole survivor" or the "toe-tally awesome doc," is the master of all things feet. Armed with a trusty magnifying glass and a toolkit that could rival a carpenter's, Dr. Stubya Toe fearlessly ventures into the land of bunions, corns, and ingrown toenails. Their superpower? They can maintain a straight face while discussing the most bizarre foot-related mishaps, from stepping on Legos to accidentally kicking the corner of the coffee table in the dead of night. So, if you're ever feeling like your feet are staging a revolt, fear not! Dr. Stubya Toe is here to put the pep back in your step and ensure that your journey through life is free from the tyranny of stubbed toes and pesky blisters!

My comments:

The "sole survivor" and the "toe-tally awesome doc" made me smile.

MY INPUT: **The urologist**

Write a humorous definition of a urologist. Name the doctor Dr. Max Flo.

ChatGPT output:

Dr. Max Flo: The urologist, also affectionately dubbed "the stream team leader" or "the bladder boss," is the intrepid explorer of the nether regions. With a stethoscope in one hand and a urine sample cup in the other, Dr. Max Flo fearlessly delves into the mysterious depths of the urinary tract. Their mission? To ensure that the plumbing system of the human body is flowing smoothly, without any leaks or clogs. Armed with a knack for awkward conversations and a collection of dad jokes that could make even the most stoic patient crack a smile, Dr. Max Flo fearlessly tackles everything from kidney stones to prostate problems. So, if you're ever feeling like your plumbing is on the fritz, fear not! Dr. Max Flo is here to ensure that your journey to the bathroom is as smooth and effortless as possible, leaving you free to conquer the world, one restroom break at a time!

My comments:

Great job. However, I was surprised at the mention of the dad jokes as they didn't seem to be related to the rest of the paragraph. However, I enjoyed the terms "the stream team leader" and the "bladder boss."

MY INPUT: **The pulmonologist**

Write a humorous definition of a pulmonologist. Name the doctor Dr. Les Breath

ChatGPT output:

Dr. Les Breath: The pulmonologist, known in medical circles as "the lung whisperer" or "the wheeze wizard," is the brave explorer of the respiratory realm. Armed with a stethoscope and a keen sense of smell (because let's face it, they've sniffed enough breath to be certified bloodhound detectives), Dr. Les Breath fearlessly ventures into the depths of coughs, wheezes, and the occasional case of smoker's lung. Their mission? To ensure that your respiratory system is functioning like a well-oiled accordion, capable of hitting all the high notes without turning blue in the face. With a knack for diagnosing the difference between a sniffle and a serious case of bronchitis, Dr. Les Breath is the unsung hero of every deep breath you take. So, if you're ever feeling like your lungs are staging a mutiny, fear not! Dr. Les Breath is here to breathe new life into your respiratory adventures, one inhalation at a time!

My comments:

Good job at humor. I especially liked the accordion analogy.

MY INPUT: The gastroenterologist

Write a humorous definition of a gastroenterologist. Name the doctor Dr. Black Scope

ChatGPT output:

Meet the gastro-guru, the colon commander, the one and only Dr. Black Scope! Armed with a flashlight brighter than your future and a scope longer than your grocery list, this fearless explorer isn't afraid to dive headfirst into the belly of the beast - quite literally. With a nose for trouble and a knack for navigating the treacherous twists and turns of your digestive highway, Dr. Black Scope fearlessly plunges into the depths of your gut, searching for answers to life's most pressing questions, like "Was it the tacos or the burritos?" and "Do beans really belong in chili?" So, if you're ever feeling like your stomach is staging a full-scale revolt, fear not! Dr. Black Scope is here to shine a light on your gut instincts and help you navigate the wild rollercoaster ride of digestion, one adventurous journey through the intestines at a time!

My comments:

This output was the second version as I asked chat to try again because the first try was on the boring side. Chat made this paragraph reasonably funny. Some might say quite funny. Chat has a problem at times with context. For example, the scope being "longer than your grocery list" is out of context. I would prefer it to have described a scope "longer than an adult anaconda" or "longer than a plumbers video snake". Somehow chat did not pick up on the long black scope with lights and knobs that the doctors use for colonoscopies and endoscopies.

MY INPUT: The infectious disease doctor

Write a humorous definition of an infectious disease doctor. Name the doctor Dr. Uben Overseas

ChatGPT output:

Dr. Uben Overseas: Welcome to the thrilling world of infectious diseases, where Dr. Uben Overseas reigns supreme as the intrepid explorer of microbial mysteries, the fearless adventurer in the realm of germs! Armed with a microscope and a passport stamped with more exotic locales than a travel blogger's dream, Dr. Uben Overseas fearlessly ventures into the microbial jungle, whether it's the depths of a tropical rainforest or the bustling streets of a foreign city. Their mission? To outsmart those sneaky pathogens and send them packing faster than you can say "bon voyage!" With a knack for diagnosing the difference between a harmless itch and a potentially deadly bite, Dr. Uben Overseas is the unsung hero of every mosquito-infested vacation and every bout of traveler's tummy. So, if you're ever feeling like you've brought back more than just souvenirs from your overseas adventures, fear not! Dr. Uben Overseas is here to fight off those pesky germs and keep you safe from the microscopic menace, no matter where your wanderlust takes you!

My comments:

This is also the output from a second try as the first try completely missed the travel and overseas element of Dr. Uben Overseas and treated the paragraph as if it were a local doctor treating a normal, non-traveling patient.

MY INPUT: The orthopedist

Write a humorous definition of an orthopedist. Name the doctor Dr. Cal Cieum

ChatGPT output:

Dr. Cal Cieum: Step into the world of bone-rattling adventures, where Dr. Cal Cieum reigns supreme as the master of all things orthopedic! With a toolkit packed full of wrenches and screws (and maybe a little WD-40 for good measure), this bone mechanic fearlessly tackles fractures, sprains, and the occasional case of "I slipped on a banana peel." Armed with X-rays and a knack for cracking jokes that are as cheesy as they come, Dr. Cal Cieum is the unsung hero of every twisted ankle and every bumpy ride down the slopes. So, if you're ever feeling like your bones are staging a rebellion, fear not! Dr. Cal Cieum is here to put the spring back in your step and ensure that your skeleton stays as sturdy as a pair of steel-toed boots, one crack at a time!

My comments:

I enjoyed the toolkit and the WD-40 reference. The final phrase "one crack at a time" did not make sense. Chat somehow pulled that phrase out of nowhere or possibly out of some construction training it encountered. It should be deleted.

MY INPUT: **The psychiatrist**

Write a humorous definition of a psychiatrist. Name the doctor Dr. Les Stress

ChatGPT output:

Dr. Les Stress: Welcome to the wild world of psychiatry, where Dr. Les Stress reigns as the mind magician, the brain whisperer, and the stress buster extraordinaire! Armed with a notepad and a couch softer than a cloud, Dr. Les Stress fearlessly dives into the labyrinth of the human psyche, navigating through dreams, fears, and the occasional Freudian slip. With a knack for deciphering the difference between a neurosis and a normal Tuesday, Dr. Les Stress is the unsung hero of every existential crisis and every "should I eat the last cookie?" dilemma. So, if you're ever feeling like your brain is doing acrobatics on a tightrope, fear not! Dr. Les Stress is here to untangle the mental mess and help you find your inner peace, one therapy session at a time!

My comments:

Good job! I especially liked the phrase "deciphering the difference between a neurosis and a normal Tuesday." Clearly chat is well informed about the world of psychiatry. The overall format of many of these descriptions starting with "welcome to the wild world of…." and finishing with a positive wrap-up is getting old.

MY INPUT: **the optometrist**

Write a humorous definition of an optometrist. Name the doctor Dr. Hardly See

ChatGPT output:

Dr. Hardly See: Step into the spectacle-filled world of optometry, where Dr. Hardly See reigns as the vision virtuoso, the sight sorcerer, and the spectacle specialist! Armed with a trusty eye chart and a collection of lenses that could rival a kaleidoscope, Dr. Hardly See fearlessly ventures into the vast expanse of your visual vortex, deciphering the mysteries of nearsightedness, farsightedness, and the occasional case of "I lost my glasses again." With a knack for distinguishing between a squint and a wink, Dr. Hardly See is the unsung hero of every blurry vision and every "are these my keys?" moment. So, if you're ever feeling like your eyes are staging a mutiny, fear not! Dr. Hardly See is here to sharpen your focus and ensure that your world stays as crystal clear as a freshly wiped lens, one blink at a time!

My comment:

This description takes me directly to my optometrist's office. Chat knows the territory! I don't know why chat added "are these my keys?" but I guess there are multiple keys in its internet scanning and training experience. I would have preferred it to express frustration with the fine print on the critical drugs such as Imodium.

MY INPUT: **The cardiologist**

Write a humorous definition of a cardiologist. Name the doctor Dr. Skip Abeat. Include in the humorous story Dr. Abeat's physician assistant Sis Tolic. Be sure to include tests such as an EKG, the dreaded treadmill stress test, and an echo cardiogram. Finally end with the scheduling dilemma that to see Dr. Abeat for the next visit it's backed up six months but to see the physician assistant you can see her next week. So much for the state of medical care these days.

ChatGPT output:

Meet Dr. Skip Abeat, the rhythm maestro of the heart, renowned cardiologist extraordinaire. With his trusty physician assistant, Sis Tolic, by his side, they navigate the cardiac seas with humor and precision.

Picture this: Mr. Heartache stumbles into Dr. Abeat's office, clutching his chest like a melodramatic actor in a soap opera. After a brief consultation and a few puns about matters of the heart, it's time for tests.

First up, the EKG – or as Dr. Abeat fondly calls it, the "Electric Kool-Aid Graph." With electrodes sticking to Mr. Heartache's chest like barnacles on a ship, they monitor the heart's electrical activity. Dr. Abeat chuckles as he reads the results, muttering something about a heart that dances to its own beat.

Then comes the dreaded treadmill stress test. As Mr. Heartache huffs and puffs like a steam engine, Dr. Abeat cheers him on, shouting motivational lines like, "You're doing great! Just a few more miles to go, or at least until lunchtime!"

Finally, it's time for the pièce de résistance – the echo cardiogram, affectionately known as the "Heart-o-Gram." Sis Tolic expertly maneuvers the ultrasound wand, capturing images of Mr. Heartache's heart in all its thumping glory. Dr. Abeat oohs and ahhs at the sight, comparing the heart's chambers to luxury hotel suites and its valves to well-oiled machinery.

But alas, all good things must come to an end, including appointments with Dr. Abeat. When Mr. Heartache tries to schedule his next visit, he's met with a scheduling dilemma of epic proportions. Dr. Abeat's calendar is booked solid for the next six months, leaving Mr. Heartache to ponder the state of medical care as he begrudgingly accepts an appointment with Sis Tolic next week.

And so, the saga of Mr. Heartache and Dr. Abeat continues, with a dash of humor and a pinch of reality, proving that even in the world of cardiology, laughter truly is the best medicine.

My comments:

Good story but I was surprised and disappointed that chat did not add anything on its own beyond my input. It might have added something about beta blocker drugs to slow the heart or common heart rhythm disorders or even something about preventing heart attacks.

MY INPUT: Today's world where children and teens live on their screens

Write a humorous story about the sad state of affairs in today's world where children and teens spend too much time on their iPhones, Android phones, and iPads. Talk about the "battle royal" between parents and their offspring about how much screen time is allowed and how this limit is enforced. Be sure to focus on lost part of a normal childhood where interpersonal skills are lost. Remember to make it funny.

ChatGPT output:

Once upon a time in the quaint town of Analogville, the local playground was a bustling haven where kids would swing, slide, and engage in the timeless ritual of tag. But as the years rolled on, Analogville was infiltrated by a mysterious force known as "The Screen." This force came in the form of shiny iPhones, sleek Android phones, and dazzling iPads. The Screen's allure was irresistible to the young inhabitants, turning them into digital zombies. Their parents, once familiar with faces flushed from running and eyes wide with wonder, were now greeted by a sea of blank expressions and the incessant tapping of tiny fingers on glass.

In the Smith household, this digital epidemic had reached critical mass. Mr. and Mrs. Smith decided it was time to wage a war—an epic "Battle Royal"—against the encroaching screens. They devised a cunning plan: a strict limit on screen time. Each child was allowed one hour a day, a decree that sent shockwaves through the Smith children, who were convinced their parents had gone completely mad.

The Smiths' eldest, Timmy, a 13-year-old who believed he was a professional gamer because he once won a game of Fortnite, was the first to rebel. He built a fort out of pillows and blankets in the living room, dubbing it "Fort-Night" and declared independence from parental rule.

He hoarded snacks and used his iPad to order reinforcements in the form of pizza delivery.

His younger sister, Sally, was equally resourceful. An aspiring social media influencer at the ripe age of 10, she began live-streaming her plight under the hashtag #FreeTheScreens, gaining a small army of digital sympathizers. Her followers suggested various strategies, including hiding the WiFi router and switching the household network to a neighbor's.

Despite the uprising, the Smith parents were undeterred. Mrs. Smith, a seasoned veteran of the Analog Era, used her secret weapon: the art of distraction. She introduced "Analog Adventures," a series of activities designed to lure the kids away from their screens. These included ancient rituals like board games, baking cookies, and the most daring of all—family walks. "It's like Pokémon GO," she explained, "but with real trees and squirrels!"

The battle reached its peak when Mr. Smith, in a moment of pure genius, hid the family's chargers. This maneuver resulted in a scene reminiscent of a zombie apocalypse movie, with Timmy and Sally desperately roaming the house, eyes glazed, murmuring, "Battery low… need power…"

Interpersonal skills, once thought to be lost forever, began to reemerge. Timmy rediscovered the joy of actual human conversation when he asked his dad for advice on building a treehouse. Sally, deprived of her virtual likes and comments, found herself laughing uncontrollably with her mom over a game of charades.

The final blow to the digital rebellion came during a family outing to the local park. Devoid of their devices, Timmy and Sally encountered other children who were also victims of the screen ban. They hesitated at first, but soon, a soccer game broke out. Real-life interactions flourished as they remembered the thrill of face-to-face competition and camaraderie.

As the sun set over Analogville, the Smiths returned home, victorious. They knew the battle wasn't over, but for now, they had reclaimed a piece of their children's childhood. The screens were still there, lurking, waiting for their moment, but the Smith family was ready. They had discovered the ultimate power-up: the strength of real-world connections and the magic of shared experiences.

And so, in the ever-ongoing Battle Royal of Analogville, the parents fought valiantly, armed with creativity, cunning, and the occasional cookie, determined to keep the spirit of childhood alive in the digital age.

My comments:

The sheer excellence of this writing blew my mind and knocked me off my chair! Wow! This was one of the last vignettes I created but I moved it toward the front of the book because it was so good. I learned the input has to be precisely and exactly targeted to what you want chat to come up with and also needs to include key ideas such as "battle royale" and the concept of lost interpersonal skills. Finally, I felt I had to add a reminder to keep it funny because it's such a serious subject and I was concerned chat might go light on the humor.

MY INPUT: The fear of missing out on AI (FOMO)

Write a humorous piece about the fear of missing out (FOMO) on AI.

ChatGPT output:

Fear of Missing Out on AI

Do you ever lie awake at night, haunted by the thought that somewhere out there, a robot is mastering calculus while you struggle to balance your checkbook? Welcome to the world of FOMO – Fear of Missing Out on AI.

It starts innocently enough. You hear about AI revolutionizing industries, creating self-driving cars, and beating grandmasters at chess. Suddenly, your toaster seems like a primitive relic from the Stone Age. You start to wonder if your microwave secretly judges your cooking skills.

As you delve deeper into the rabbit hole of artificial intelligence, FOMO sinks its teeth in. You imagine a future where Siri and Alexa have formed a secret society, discussing philosophy and plotting the downfall of humanity, while you're still trying to figure out how to set a reminder on your phone.

Every news headline about AI breakthroughs feels like a personal attack on your intelligence. You start to panic-buy books with titles like "AI for Dummies" and "Machine Learning Made Easy," hoping to catch up before the robots take over.

But as you struggle through page after page of complex algorithms and neural networks, you realize that maybe, just maybe, AI isn't for everyone. Maybe you're better off leaving the future of technology to the experts while you focus on more important things, like perfecting your pancake recipe or finally learning how to fold a fitted sheet.

And so, armed with a newfound sense of self-awareness (and a healthy dose of humor), you embrace your FOMO and wear it like a badge of honor. Because while the robots may be taking over the world, at least you'll always have your human quirks – like the ability to laugh at yourself, even in the face of impending AI doom.

My comments:

It would be nice if chat had added a little more about people's real fears of missing out. Many people instantly think about the extreme negative effects of AI rather than a balanced approach covering both negative and positive effects of AI.

MY INPUT: Give a non-techy description of how ChatGPT works

Explain how ChatGPT 3.5 works from the point of view of a *layperson*, a non-techy person. Please use absolutely as much humor as possible.

ChatGPT output:

Alrighty, let's break down ChatGPT 3.5 in a way even your grandma's pet goldfish could understand. Picture this: you're sitting at your computer, scratching your head and pondering life's deepest questions like "Why do we park in driveways and drive on parkways?" Suddenly, a wild thought appears: "I wish I had someone to chat with about this!"

Enter ChatGPT 3.5, the ultimate chatty buddy that's like having a brainy best friend trapped inside your computer. It's like Siri, but with a PhD in witty banter and a penchant for puns. You type in your burning question, and faster than you can say "knock-knock joke," ChatGPT is there with a clever response that'll have you rolling on the floor laughing.

But how does this magical marvel of modern technology work, you ask? Well, imagine a giant library filled with every book, article, and internet meme ever written. Now, imagine that library is actually a super-smart computer that's spent its entire existence devouring all that knowledge and storing it in its digital brain. That's ChatGPT 3.5 in a nutshell.

When you type a question or message into ChatGPT, it sifts through its vast library of information faster than a librarian on caffeine. It analyzes your words, sprinkles in a dash of algorithmic magic, and voila! You've got yourself a witty reply that's as entertaining as it is informative. It's like having a conversation with the Encyclopedia Britannica, but way less boring and way more sassy.

Now, let's talk about the fun part: humor. ChatGPT 3.5 isn't just a boring old robot spouting off facts like a walking Wikipedia page. Oh no, my friend, it's a veritable stand-up comedian trapped in a computer's body. It'll crack jokes, tell puns, and even drop a well-timed meme or two just to keep you entertained.

So whether you're pondering the meaning of life, debating the best flavor of ice cream, or just looking for someone to share your cat memes with, ChatGPT 3.5 is your go-to buddy for all things hilarious and informative. Just remember to thank your computer for the laughs—it's working hard to keep you entertained, one witty comeback at a time.

My comments:

Excellent description however I was quite surprised at the amount of humor chat came up with. The phrase, ". . . it's a veritable stand-up comedian trapped in a computer's body" was "creative". I initially hesitated to use the word "creative" as I am not sure, technically, you can use that word when discussing the output of chat. The illusion of being "creative"?

•

MY INPUT: Give a technical description of how ChatGPT works

Now write a very humorous, short, *technical* description of how ChatGPT 3.5 works

ChatGPT output:

ChatGPT 3.5 is an advanced language model developed by OpenAI. It works by processing input text and generating coherent and contextually relevant responses based on its extensive training on a diverse dataset of text from the internet. Using deep learning techniques, ChatGPT 3.5 analyzes the input text, identifies patterns, and generates responses that mimic human-like conversation. Its capabilities are powered by a large neural network architecture that enables it to understand and generate natural language text.

My comments:

Chat overlooked the input request asking for humor, but the output was splendidly short and to the point. Could it be chat knew that humor and technical descriptions are antithetical?

MY INPUT: **A visit to the dentist**

Write a humorous story about what it's like to go to the dentist to get your teeth cleaned. Include a full range of human emotions. Cover the following items: The contour dental chair looks quite comfortable but had a hard uncomfortable headrest that's built for a person that's 6'3" tall. You had to swish for 60 seconds with a horrible tasting antiseptic to kill any possible Covid viruses. You had to endure an ultrasonic cleaning device that emits ear splitting annoying, high frequency sounds at 110 DB. You came within a split second of a perceived waterboard death because the little suction tube didn't suck up saliva fast enough. You had to endure the effects of a surgical steel instrument that scraped your teeth emitting an annoying high-pitched sound. Could it be the dental hygienist remembered the horrible screeching sound chalk sometimes makes on a blackboard and wanted you to experience the same thing? Finally, the polishing step—a rotating little brush polished each tooth using a compound with a grit that seemed to come from the local beach.

ChatGPT output:

Going to the dentist can be an experience akin to navigating a treacherous obstacle course, and today was no exception. I had bravely signed up for my routine teeth cleaning, blissfully unaware of the emotional rollercoaster that awaited me.

As I entered the pristine dental office, I was greeted by a contour dental chair that looked like it belonged in a luxury spa. "Looks comfy," I thought, taking my seat. That thought quickly vanished as my head met the headrest, clearly designed for someone around 6'3". My neck was contorted at an angle that would make a yoga instructor proud.

Next, the dental hygienist, a cheerful woman with a smile that seemed just a bit too enthusiastic, handed me a small cup. "Swish this for 60 seconds," she chirped. The liquid tasted like a concoction of old gym socks and battery acid. Apparently, this vile substance was designed to kill any possible Covid viruses lurking in my mouth. I swished, gagged, and tried not to lose my breakfast.

With the preliminaries out of the way, the hygienist wielded the ultrasonic cleaning device like a conductor preparing for a symphony. She turned it on, and my ears were assaulted by high-frequency sounds that could summon dolphins from miles away. The noise reached a mind-numbing 110 decibels. I began to wonder if this was some form of secret dental revenge for all the candy I'd consumed.

As if the sound wasn't enough, I suddenly found myself in a near-death experience. The little suction tube designed to remove saliva decided to go on strike. My mouth flooded, and for a brief, terrifying moment, I felt like I was being waterboarded. I flailed and gurgled until the hygienist, noticing my distress, calmly adjusted the tube. Crisis averted, but my heart was still racing.

Just as I started to recover, she picked up a surgical steel instrument that looked like it belonged in a medieval torture chamber. As she scraped my teeth, it emitted a high-pitched sound that could have been the soundtrack to a horror film. I couldn't help but wonder if she had once been a schoolteacher with a vendetta against chalkboards. The screech was identical to nails on a chalkboard, and it reverberated through my very soul.

Finally, we reached the polishing step. "This is the easy part," she assured me, as she prepared the rotating brush. I relaxed slightly, only to discover that the polishing compound had the texture of gritty sand. I was pretty sure they had sourced it from the nearest beach. The little brush whirred and buzzed, scrubbing each tooth with enthusiastic fervor. By the time it was over, my teeth felt polished, but my mouth felt like it had been through a sandstorm.

When it was all said and done, I staggered out of the dental chair, my emotions a tangled mess. Relief, exhaustion, and the faintest hint of pride swirled within me. I had survived the dentist! As I left the office, the hygienist handed me a new toothbrush and a small tube of toothpaste as consolation prizes. "See you in six months!" she called cheerily.

Six months? I thought. Maybe I'd just switch to a liquid diet instead.

My comments:

This chat output was incredibly good! This may be chat at its best—probably due to the more accurate detailed input and the "knowledge" level chat has about the dental world.

MY INPUT: The top 10 musical stars, including Taylor Swift

List the top 10 musical stars, including people like Beyoncé and Taylor Swift

ChatGPT output

As of my last update in January 2022, here are ten of the top musical stars, including Beyoncé and Taylor Swift:

Beyoncé
Taylor Swift
Drake
Ariana Grande
Ed Sheeran
Justin Bieber
Adele
Rihanna
Billie Eilish
Post Malone

Please note that popularity and rankings can change over time, so it's always a good idea to check the latest charts and updates for the most current information.

My comments:

Looks like an excellent list. I'm pleased Beyoncé and Taylor Swift were at the top of the list.

MY INPUT: **Write a humorous explanation of each star**

Now write an extremely humorous explanation of each star and their type of performance *to retired people in their mid 80s*.

ChatGPT output

Alright, let's take a whimsical trip down memory lane and explain these musical stars to retired folks in their mid-80s, shall we?

Beyoncé: Imagine the most dazzling performer you've ever seen at the local talent show, then multiply that by a million. Beyoncé is like the queen of music, ruling over her kingdom with a voice that could make angels jealous and dance moves that defy the laws of physics. If you haven't heard of her, just picture your grandkids trying to imitate her fierce strut while lip-syncing into their hairbrushes.

Taylor Swift: Picture your granddaughter's diary brought to life through catchy tunes and heartbreak anthems. Taylor Swift is like the modern-day Shakespeare of love songs, turning every romantic mishap into a chart-topping hit. Whether she's singing about her latest breakup or her favorite cat, you can bet your bottom dollar there's a Taylor Swift song for every mood.

Drake: Imagine your grandson's favorite rapper, but with a softer side and an affinity for emotional vulnerability. Drake is like the sensitive soul of the hip-hop world, pouring his heart out over smooth beats and infectious hooks. He's the kind of guy who could make you shed a tear one minute and then have you dancing in your rocking chair the next.

Ariana Grande: Picture the petite powerhouse with a ponytail higher than your pension, belting out high notes like it's nobody's business. Ariana Grande is like the modern-day diva, channeling the spirit of Mariah Carey with a sprinkle of sass and a whole lot of vocal acrobatics. If you've ever heard your great-granddaughter practicing her whistle tones in the shower, you can thank Ariana for that.

Ed Sheeran: Imagine your grandson's scruffy best friend who always shows up to family gatherings with his guitar in tow. Ed Sheeran is like the boy next door who serenades you with heartfelt ballads about love, life, and everything in between. With his ginger locks and soulful crooning, he's the kind of guy you'd want to invite over for tea and a sing-along.

Justin Bieber: Think back to that charming troublemaker from your high school days, then add millions of screaming fans and a penchant for catchy pop tunes. Justin Bieber is like the boy wonder of the music industry, transforming from teen heartthrob to grown-up crooner right before our eyes. If you've ever wondered why your granddaughter has "Bieber Fever," just imagine Elvis Presley with a modern-day makeover.

Adele: Picture your granddaughter's favorite torch singer, but with a British accent and enough soul to make Aretha Franklin proud. Adele is like the voice of a generation, belting out power ballads that speak to the depths of the human experience. If you've ever found yourself reaching for the tissues while listening to the radio, chances are Adele was the one tugging at your heartstrings.

Rihanna: Imagine the ultimate fashion icon strutting down the runway, then throw in a killer voice and a rebellious attitude to boot. Rihanna is like the bad girl of pop music, flipping the script on what it means to be a modern-day diva. Whether she's singing about umbrella-ellas or shining bright like a diamond, she's got a style and swagger all her own.

Billie Eilish: Picture your granddaughter's edgy friend who always marches to the beat of her own drum, then add a haunting voice and a wardrobe straight out of a Tim Burton film. Billie Eilish is like the dark princess of pop, enchanting audiences with her whispery vocals and brooding lyrics. If you've ever wondered what the kids these days are listening to, just imagine Lana Del Rey with a touch of teenage angst.

Post Malone: Imagine your grandson's favorite rapper, but with a love for tattoos and a penchant for country twang. Post Malone is like the musical chameleon of our generation, blending hip-hop, rock, and even a little bit of folk into his signature sound. With his laid-back vibe and infectious charm, he's the kind of guy you'd want to invite over for a barbecue and a jam session.

So, there you have it, folks! A humorous crash course in modern-day musical royalty, tailor-made for the retired crowd in their mid-80s. Whether you're tapping your toes to Beyoncé or shedding a tear to Adele, one thing's for sure: music has a way of transcending generations and bringing us all together, one catchy chorus at a time.

My comments:

One of the best performances by chat! Chat sure knows popular singers.

MY INPUT: **TV Drug Ads**

Write a satire of tv drug ads including all the terrible side effects such as difficulty breathing, blindness and death! Ridicule drugs for minor ailments that heretofore are not very well known but promoted because big pharma found a drug that helped them.

ChatGPT output:

[Scene: A brightly lit living room. A cheerful jingle plays as the camera zooms in on a family gathered around the TV.]

Voiceover: "Are you tired of feeling slightly uncomfortable? Introducing HypoWell™, the revolutionary new medication for the condition you never knew you had!"

[Cut to a smiling family enjoying outdoor activities.]

Voiceover: "With HypoWell™, you'll forget you ever suffered from Mild Discomfort Syndrome (MDS)! Say goodbye to those pesky, barely noticeable symptoms like occasional sniffles or indigestion."

[Quick montage of people struggling with everyday tasks like tying shoelaces or opening jars.]

Voiceover: "But don't take our word for it! Listen to these satisfied customers."

[Cut to testimonials from actors with exaggerated expressions of relief.]

Actor 1: "Before HypoWell™, I didn't even know I had a problem!"

Actor 2: "Thanks to HypoWell™, I can now live my life without the burden of feeling slightly off!"

Voiceover: "But wait, there's more! Along with the miraculous relief from (MDS), you may experience some minor side effects."

[Text flashes on the screen in tiny font as the voiceover speaks rapidly.]

Voiceover: "Side effects may include but are not limited to: nausea, dizziness, headaches, blurred vision, loss of appetite, increased urge to yell at your children, insomnia, triple vision, mood swings, uncontrollable laughter, a distaste for chocolate, difficulty breathing, sudden urge to speak in rhymes, constant desire to order dinner out and permeant blindness, and death."

[Cut to the family from earlier, still smiling but now engaged in activities while dealing with the absurd side effects.]

Voiceover: "Ask your doctor if HypoWell™ is right for you. Side effects may vary. Do not take HypoWell™ if you are allergic to feeling better or if you have a history of smiling."

[The jingle returns as the screen fades to black.]

Voiceover: "HypoWell™: Because why settle for feeling normal when you can feel absolutely mediocre."

My comments:

This story required extremely minor edits to the "side effects" paragraph to make the list longer. However, chat did a compelling, captivating and marvelous job and obviously knows drug commercials.

MY INPUT: The most useful aspects of ChatGPT

What are the top seven most useful aspects of chat GDP

ChatGPT output:

Certainly! Here are seven of the most useful aspects of ChatGPT:

Information Retrieval: ChatGPT can quickly provide information on a wide range of topics, making it a valuable resource for answering questions and seeking clarification.

Language Comprehension: ChatGPT understands and processes natural language input, allowing for more conversational interactions compared to traditional search engines.

Personalized Assistance: ChatGPT can tailor responses based on context, providing personalized assistance and recommendations to users.

translation services.

Educational Tool: ChatGPT can serve as an educational tool, helping users learn about complex topics in a conversational manner.

Entertainment: ChatGPT can engage users with entertaining conversations, jokes, and stories, making it a versatile and enjoyable tool for leisure time.

These aspects make ChatGPT a valuable resource for a wide range of users, from students and professionals seeking information to individuals looking for entertainment and companionship.

Creativity and Problem-Solving: ChatGPT's ability to generate text allows it to offer creative solutions to problems and brainstorm ideas on various subjects.

Language Translation: ChatGPT can facilitate communication across language barriers by providing real-time

My comments:

This is an impressive list of chat capabilities and its usefulness in everyday life and in business.

MY INPUT: A humorous article about the most useful aspects of ChatGPT

Write a humorous article about the most recent seven aspects of ChatGPT. Don't start with the usual beginning of the story that in once upon a time and sometimes something was happening.

ChatGPT output

The Magnificent Seven: Hilarious Highlights of the Latest ChatGPT Features

The Sherlock Holmes Mode: Ever felt like you needed a detective to untangle your messy conversations? Fear not! ChatGPT now comes with a built-in Sherlock Holmes mode, where it not only understands what you're saying but also deduces your intentions with uncanny accuracy. It's like having your very own digital detective, minus the deerstalker hat.

The Shakespearean Insult Generator: Tired of the same old insults? ChatGPT's got your back with its new Shakespearean Insult Generator feature. Whether you need to put a pompous colleague in their place or roast your best friend in style, ChatGPT will craft insults so eloquent, they'll make Shakespeare himself blush (or roll over in his grave).

The Emoji Translator: For those moments when words just aren't enough, ChatGPT now boasts an Emoji Translator feature. Simply type in your favorite emoji, and ChatGPT will translate it into a beautifully crafted sentence worthy of an emoji-themed poetry slam. 🎭💬

The Fortune Teller Mode: Curious about your future? ChatGPT now doubles as a fortune teller with its Fortune Teller Mode. Just ask a question about your destiny, and prepare to be amazed as ChatGPT predicts your future with eerie accuracy. Disclaimer: Results may vary. Consult a real fortune teller for serious inquiries.

The Comedian Bot: Need a good laugh? Look no further than ChatGPT's new Comedian Bot feature. With its vast database of jokes and witty comebacks, ChatGPT will have you rolling on the floor laughing in no time. Just be prepared for some seriously pun-ishing humor.

The Mind Reader: Ever wish someone could read your mind? ChatGPT's got you covered with its Mind Reader feature. Just think of a question, and ChatGPT will magically provide the answer. It's like having a psychic hotline, minus the questionable legitimacy.

The Virtual Therapist: Feeling stressed? ChatGPT now offers virtual therapy sessions with its Virtual Therapist feature. Pour your heart out to ChatGPT, and watch as it dispenses sage advice and comforting words of wisdom. Who needs a human therapist when you have a virtual one that never judges your life choices?

With these new features, ChatGPT is not just a language model – it's a multi-talented entertainer, problem solver, and confidant all rolled into one. Who knew artificial intelligence could be so hilariously human?

My comments:

Chat continues to amaze me. I am surprised to see this much humor coming from chat. Sometimes it seems humorless and other times it seems to have a sense of humor. For example the terms "Fortune Teller Mode" and "Virtual Therapist" were enjoyable.

MY INPUT: The 10 most important factors for college admission

List the 10 most important factors for college admission. List items such as the admission essay, the selection of a college, the importance of high school grades, the importance of extracurricular activities, and the importance of other leadership activities.

ChatGPT output:

Admission Essay: A compelling and well-written admission essay that showcases the applicant's unique qualities, experiences, and aspirations.

Selection of College: Demonstrating genuine interest in and alignment with the values, programs, and opportunities offered by the college.

High School Grades: Strong academic performance throughout high school, including rigorous coursework and a solid GPA.

Extracurricular Activities: Active participation and leadership roles in extracurricular activities such as clubs, sports, volunteer work, or part-time jobs.

Letters of Recommendation: Positive and insightful letters of recommendation from teachers, mentors, or community leaders who can attest to the applicant's character and abilities.

Standardized Test Scores: SAT or ACT scores that meet or exceed the college's expectations and demonstrate academic readiness.

Personal Achievements: Notable achievements or awards in academic, artistic, athletic, or other areas that highlight the applicant's talents and dedication.

Demonstrated Interest: Engagement with the college through campus visits, interviews, attending information sessions, or contacting admissions representatives.

Diversity and Inclusion: Contributions to diversity and inclusion initiatives or experiences that enhance the college community.

Demonstrated Leadership: Evidence of leadership skills through positions of responsibility, initiative-taking, or impactful projects within school or community organizations.

My comments:

Excellent, impressive list.

MY INPUT: **The dreaded college admission process**

Write a long humorous and comical story using the above list of college entrance items. Talk about all the emotions the student experiences, the ups and downs, all the fears, the fear of not getting into the "right school" (Harvard, Duke, or Stanford?), the fear of not being with friends. Be sure to make it humorous because these are difficult issues. Cover the wide range of emotions because these are wonderful times being a high school junior or senior. The senior prom and senior pranks and ditch day should not be clouded with all the worry about getting into the right school and completing the difficult admissions process. Give some humorous examples of senior pranks. It's a wonderful time of life not to be dominated by college admissions. Finish up the humorous story by fast forwarding 10 years and showing the student being successful, possibly with a family and children and a reasonably good job. What is more important, being successful in life or getting into absolutely the right school while creating gallons of stomach acid sweating over perfecting the admissions process?

And it's all about balance in life and college admission time tends to swing the pendulum way out of balance.

ChatGPT output:

Once upon a time, in the bustling halls of Roosevelt High School, there was a student named Sam. Now, Sam wasn't your average high schooler; he was a whirlwind of emotions wrapped up in a chaotic ball of nerves, particularly when it came to the dreaded college admissions process.

It all began innocently enough in his junior year when Sam's guidance counselor handed him a brochure filled with glossy images of ivy-covered buildings and smiling students. "It's time to start thinking about college," the counselor chirped, unaware of the existential crisis that was about to befall poor Sam.

The first hurdle was the admission essay. Sam spent countless nights staring at a blank computer screen, grappling with existential questions like, "Who am I?" and "What do I want out of life?" They eventually settled on a topic—the profound impact of his pet goldfish on his worldview. It was either that or a treatise on the philosophical implications of SpongeBob SquarePants.

Next came the selection of a college. Harvard, Duke, Stanford—the names sent shivers down Sam's spine. The pressure to get into one of these prestigious institutions was immense. Every decision he made seemed to hinge on the belief that his entire future depended on getting into the "right" school.

But amidst the chaos of college prep, there were moments of levity. Senior prom was a magical night filled with awkward dance moves and questionable fashion choices. And then there were the senior pranks— oh, the senior pranks. Sam and his friends once released a herd of goats into the school cafeteria, causing chaos that would be talked about for years to come.

Yet, looming over these moments of joy was the constant fear of rejection. What if Sam didn't get into their dream school? What if he ended up miles away from his friends? The thought of spending four years surrounded by strangers was enough to induce a panic attack.

But as fate would have it, Sam's hard work paid off, and he was accepted into their top choice college. As he walked across the stage at graduation, clutching his diploma like a lifeline, he realized something important: life was about more than just getting into the "right" school.

Fast forward ten years, and Sam is thriving. He has a loving family, a fulfilling career, and a sense of peace that comes from knowing that success isn't measured by the name on your diploma. It's measured by the laughter of your children, the love of your partner, and the memories you make along the way.

So, to all the high schoolers out there sweating over college admissions, remember this: it's okay to stress, it's okay to worry, but don't let the process consume you. In the grand scheme of things, what matters most is not where you go to college, but what you do with the opportunities life throws your way.

My comments:

The phrase about the herd of goats in the school cafeteria was delightful as was the prom comment, ". . . questionable fashion choices." Chat followed the input fairly well."

MY INPUT: **Going through airport security**

What are the 10 steps required to go through airport security?

ChatGPT output:

The specific steps can vary slightly depending on the airport and security procedures, but generally, here are the 10 steps required to go through airport security:

Check-In: Present your boarding pass and identification at the airline check-in counter or kiosk.

Baggage Screening: Place your carry-on luggage and personal items on the conveyor belt for X-ray screening.

Document Check: Show your boarding pass and identification to the TSA agent at the security checkpoint.

Remove Outerwear: Take off coats, jackets, belts, and any bulky outerwear.

Empty Pockets: Empty your pockets of all items and place them in a bin for X-ray screening.

Remove Electronics: Take out laptops, tablets, cameras, and other large electronics and place them in a separate bin.

Remove Liquids: Take out any liquids, gels, and aerosols from your carry-on bag and place them in a clear, plastic bag.

Pass Through Security Scanner: Walk through the metal detector or full-body scanner.

Wait for Baggage Screening: Wait for your carry-on items to go through the X-ray machine while you proceed through the security scanner.

Gather Belongings: Retrieve your belongings from the X-ray screening area and proceed to your departure gate.

It's important to follow instructions from TSA agents and be prepared to comply with additional security measures if required.

MY INPUT:

Please write a humorous article related to these checklist items going through security. Concentrate on showing the frustration and emotion at each step of the way.

ChatGPT output

The Great Airport Security Shuffle: A Humorous Journey Through Checkpoint Chaos

Ah, the joys of airport security! It's like a game show where the prize is getting to your gate without losing your sanity. As travelers, we've all experienced the rollercoaster of emotions that come with navigating the labyrinthine process of passing through the hallowed halls of TSA. So, let's embark on a comical expedition through the 10 stages of airport security, where frustration and emotion reign supreme.

Check-In:

You approach the check-in counter with all the optimism of a kid at Disneyland, only to be greeted by a line longer than the Great Wall of China. Your enthusiasm takes a nosedive as you watch the clock ticking closer to your departure time. "Sure, I'll just sprint to the gate," you mutter under your breath, already dreading the impending marathon.

Baggage Screening:

As you shuffle towards the X-ray machine, you're struck by the realization that you've packed enough electronics to rival a Best Buy store. You watch in horror as your meticulously organized carry-on transforms into a chaotic jumble of cables and gadgets. "Maybe I should've just brought a typewriter," you lament, mentally preparing for the inevitable TSA agent's raised eyebrow.

Document Check:

With boarding pass and ID in hand, you approach the TSA agent like a weary traveler seeking refuge in an oasis. But alas, your dreams of a smooth passage are shattered when you realize your boarding pass is hiding in the abyss of your backpack. After a frantic search that rivals a scene from Indiana Jones, you emerge victorious, albeit slightly disheveled.

Remove Outerwear:

Stripping down to your skivvies in the middle of the security checkpoint, you can't help but wonder if this is the latest installment of a hidden camera prank show. With each layer shed, your dignity diminishes, until you're left feeling more exposed than a contestant on a reality TV dating show.

Empty Pockets:

You approach the conveyor belt with all the confidence of a seasoned traveler, only to realize you've forgotten to empty your pockets. As you frantically dump loose change, keys, and a half-eaten granola bar into the bin, you can't help but feel like a magician performing a failed disappearing act.

Remove Electronics:

Laptops, tablets, cameras—oh my! You watch in horror as your beloved gadgets are subjected to the merciless scrutiny of the X-ray machine.

"Please be gentle," you whisper, silently praying that your laptop survives the journey unscathed. After all, you have a high-stakes game of solitaire waiting for you on the other side.

Remove Liquids:

Ah, the dreaded liquid rule. As you dig through your bag for that pesky travel-sized shampoo, you can't help but wonder if TSA agents moonlight as bathroom product aficionados. With each bottle scrutinized like a priceless artifact, you can't help but question the absurdity of a world where a bottle of toothpaste is considered a potential threat.

Pass Through Security Scanner:

With your dignity in tatters and your belongings scattered to the winds, you take a deep breath and step into the abyss of the security scanner. As the machine whirs and clicks around you, you can't shake the feeling that you've stumbled into a sci-fi movie set. "Beam me up, Scotty," you joke nervously, hoping for a smooth passage to the other side.

Wait for Baggage Screening:

With baited breath, you watch as your belongings inch their way through the X-ray machine. Each passing second feels like an eternity, until finally, the conveyor belt comes to a halt. With a sigh of relief, you prepare to reclaim your scattered treasures and make a break for the nearest Starbucks.

Gather Belongings:

As you gather your belongings from the conveyor belt, you can't help but marvel at the sheer absurdity of the past few minutes. "Well, that was an adventure," you chuckle to yourself, vowing to pack lighter and arrive earlier next time. With your sanity intact (barely), you set off towards your gate, ready to tackle whatever airport shenanigans come your way.

And so concludes our comedic odyssey through the whimsical world of airport security. Remember, dear traveler, in the face of chaos and frustration, laughter is truly the best medicine. Until next time, happy travels, and may your journeys be as entertaining as they are enlightening!

My comments:

Chat gets it! Obviously, chat is a frequent flyer. Chat did make a subtle sequence/context error (hallucination) where it put the baggage screening via X-ray before the document check. Just proves eagle eye proof reading is required.

MY INPUT: The over accomplished family holiday letter

Holiday letter 2023. It was an excellent year for our family. Ed is in high school, Alice is in sixth grade, Bud is in first grade, and Susan and I are barely growing older. Ed was named valedictorian and voted the most likely to succeed and spent spring break helping build a house in Quito, Ecuador. He was admitted to Harvard because he was a skateboard champion. Alice was named the star of the soccer team, her water polo team, her basketball team, her field hockey team, and her rugby team. Bud, our family geek, built an AI robot that won the US National Title. His robot could scramble eggs and throw a frisbee 75 yards. Susan was president of the PTA, a school board observer, and was awarded a gift certificate to Nordstrom's for her volunteering in the classroom. I received a giant promotion that brought me closer to being the executive VP at my company. In addition, I won the top golf award at the club and was runner up in the club tennis tournament. All in all it was a year to be remembered, accomplishments abound for the whole family. Peace, Joy and Love to all

ChatGPT output:

Holiday Letter 2023

Greetings, friends and family!

Hold onto your sleigh bells because you're in for a ride through the rollercoaster of our year! 2023 has been a whirlwind of hilarity, hijinks, and the occasional high-five-worthy moment for our family. Let me break it down for you:

Ed, our resident brainiac, not only aced high school but also snagged the titles of valedictorian and "most likely to succeed". Who knew that his secret to success would involve both textbooks and skateboards? Oh, and did I mention he spent his spring break in Ecuador building houses? Yep, he's basically a modern-day Renaissance man.

Meanwhile, Alice, our sports superstar, has been dominating the field like it's her personal playground. Soccer, water polo, basketball, field hockey, rugby - you name it, she's the MVP. We're pretty sure she's secretly cloning herself to play on all these teams, but we'll let you in on that little secret later.

Now, let's talk about Bud, our family geek extraordinaire. This kid built a robot that not only won the US National Title but also has some serious culinary and frisbee-throwing skills. Move over, Iron Man, there's a new tech superhero in town, and he's armed with scrambled eggs and frisbees.

Susan, aka the queen of multitasking, has been ruling the PTA, the school board, and basically anything else that involves volunteering. Her reward? A gift certificate to Nordstrom's, because even superheroes need a little retail therapy sometimes.

As for me, well, let's just say I've been climbing the corporate ladder one golf swing at a time. Oh, and did I mention I'm a runner-up in the club tennis tournament? Yeah, turns out my backhand is almost as impressive as my ability to delegate tasks at work.

In summary, 2023 has been a year filled with laughter, love, and more than a few eyebrow-raising moments. As we gather around this holiday season, let's raise a glass to another year of hilarity and hijinks. Happy Holidays and Happy New Year, everyone!

Cheers,

[Your Name]

My comments:

Chat deleted specifics such as "throw a frisbee 75 yards" and replaced it with "frisbee-throwing skills". This waters down the humor and makes the output somewhat bland. Chat confused the context with the new superhero as it said he was armed with scrambled eggs and frisbees, however the eggs and frisbees were characteristics of the robot and not Bud. This looks like "context confusion". Also, the phrase, "Move over, Iron Man . . .." implies a person and not a robot.

MY INPUT: **The difficulty of filling out your income tax**

Why is filling out your income tax so difficult?

ChatGPT output:

Filling out income tax can be difficult for several reasons:

Complexity of Tax Laws: Tax codes are intricate and frequently updated, making it challenging to keep up with the latest rules and regulations.

Variety of Forms: There are many different forms and schedules, each with specific requirements and purposes, which can be confusing to navigate.

Detailed Documentation Required: Gathering and organizing all necessary documents, such as income statements, deductions, and credits, can be time-consuming and overwhelming.

Varied Income Sources: Different types of income (e.g., salary, freelance, investments) are taxed differently, requiring multiple forms and calculations.

Deductions and Credits: Understanding and applying eligible deductions and credits correctly requires careful attention to detail and knowledge of tax laws.

Errors and Penalties: The fear of making mistakes that could lead to penalties or audits adds pressure and complexity to the process.

Software and Tools: While tax software can simplify the process, learning how to use these tools effectively still requires some effort and understanding.

State and Local Variations: Different states and localities have their own tax rules, which adds another layer of complexity for those who need to file multiple returns.

Self-Employment and Small Business: Taxes for self-employed individuals and small business owners involve additional forms and calculations, such as estimating quarterly taxes and managing business expenses.

Changing Personal Situations: Life changes like marriage, having children, buying a home, or retirement can significantly impact tax filings, requiring adjustments and new forms.

My comments:

Excellent list. No wonder I dislike filling out my taxes. This chat output will be used for input to the next chat request. Using chat to input to chat is an enormous productivity boost.

MY INPUT: The difficulty of filling out your income tax

Write a humorous story about the frustrations of filling out income tax forms, based on the above 10 items. Make sure you emphasize the fear of making a mistake and the chasing down of documents that you absolutely can't find.

ChatGPT output:

Once upon a tax season, in the quaint suburb of Deductionville, lived a man named Harold who dreaded one thing more than losing his TV remote: filling out his income tax. Harold's adventure began with a mountain of forms, an abyss of receipts, and a haunted drawer of missing documents.

Harold sat at his dining table, which had morphed into Tax Central. He stared at the W-2s, 1099s, and a plethora of other cryptic forms, each seemingly designed to test his sanity. "Alright, Harold," he muttered to himself, "let's tackle this beast."

His first quest was to find his Social Security card. He rummaged through drawers, old shoeboxes, and even the cookie jar. Alas, it was nowhere to be found. Instead, he discovered an expired gym membership and a coupon for 10% off laundry detergent. "Great," he grumbled, "I can lift weights and have clean clothes, but I still can't fill out my taxes."

Next, Harold needed his previous year's tax return. It was stored in a 'safe place'—a place so safe that even Harold couldn't find it. After an hour of frantic searching, he unearthed a pile of old Christmas cards and a box of novelty socks. "Who knew tax season was so festive?" he sighed.

Then came the hunt for proof of expenses. Harold had kept every receipt… somewhere. His house turned into a whirlwind of paper. Receipts for everything from groceries to dog grooming flew about. His cat, Mr. Whiskers, leaped into the chaos, shredding a particularly important looking one. "Thanks, Whiskers. I'm sure the IRS will understand."

With a frazzled mind, Harold tackled his investment income. The 1099 forms were mysteriously absent. He called his investment firm, only to be greeted by a symphony of hold music. By the time a human voice answered, Harold had learned three new instrumental versions of "Eye of the Tiger."

Mortgage interest statements and state tax records were next on the list. "Piece of cake," he thought. But the cake was a lie. The mortgage statement was buried under a pile of unfiled mail, and the state tax records had seemingly been transported to another dimension.

In the midst of this turmoil, Harold remembered his childcare expenses. He dialed the daycare, hoping for a quick response. Instead, he was subjected to an impromptu parent-teacher conference about his toddler's fondness for eating crayons. "Couldn't this wait until after tax season?" he groaned.

Harold's fear of making a mistake was palpable. Every form, every box ticked, felt like a step closer to an audit. He envisioned stern IRS agents, in dark suits and sunglasses, ready to pounce on any minor error. His hands trembled as he double-checked and triple-checked every entry.

Finally, after days of chaos and an emotional rollercoaster that rivaled any soap opera, Harold sat back. His tax return was complete, or so he hoped. He clicked 'Submit' with the same trepidation as defusing a bomb.

A week later, Harold received an email. He opened it with bated breath. "Congratulations, your tax return has been accepted." He let out a triumphant laugh, startling Mr. Whiskers.

Harold vowed to be better organized next year. But deep down, he knew that come next tax season, he'd embark on another epic quest through the labyrinth of forms, receipts, and misplaced documents. And maybe, just maybe, he'd find that elusive Social Security card.

My comments:

Chat's fixation on the Social Security card doesn't make sense, especially because the Social Security number is on the W-2 form and on last year's tax forms (once they are found). Also, many people rarely use their actual Social Security card but just keep the SS number on file or have it memorized.

There's a sequence inconsistency (logical or context error?) because in paragraph two it says ". . .. stared at the 1099s" but later chat says, "The 1099 forms were mysteriously absent." Chat evidently has a weakness in the income tax area. I completely rejected an earlier attempt where I asked chat to write a humorous story about income tax and chat seemed to not understand several of the financial expressions and tax terms. Chat will never become a CPA!

The clever phrase, "... his toddler's fondness for eating crayons." shows chats ability to add humor. Looks like chat truly understands preschool. Shouldn't we give chat a break as preschool is much more interesting than income taxes?

MY INPUT: **3D printing**

Special background note: Chat can create poetry such as love poems and poems about the beauty of flowers and the like. I thought I would challenge chat by asking it to create a poem about a technical subject—3D printing. As many readers may already know, 3D printing is now extremely popular even among children using low-cost home 3D printers for hobby projects such as creating toys and holiday decorations such as Halloween ghosts.

MY INPUT: **3-D printing**

List the top 20 items related to 3-D printing

ChatGPT output:

Sure, here are the top 20 items related to 3-D printing:

3D printers
Filament (PLA, ABS, PETG, etc.)
Resin
Print beds
Nozzles
Build plates
Print removal tools
Print cooling fans
Print surface adhesives
3D modeling software
Slicers (software)
Print bed leveling tools
Calibration tools
Print enclosure kits
Print monitoring cameras
Filament dryers

Post-processing tools (sanding, painting, etc.)
Print cleaning tools (for resin prints)
Dual-extruder kits
Print bed heaters

MY INPUT: 3-D printing

Create a humorous poem of 3-D printing, including above 20 items

ChatGPT output

In the realm of 3-D printing delight,
Where dreams take form in layers bright,
A filament spool, a wizard's wand,
Creates wonders grand, beyond despond.

With printers tall, and nozzles fine,
Resin pools like magic wine,
Build plates await their structured fate,
As models emerge, oh so great!

But beware the bed that's not quite flat,
For prints can warp, oh, what a spat!
Yet fear not, for leveling tools abound,
To ensure each layer's properly crowned.

Cooling fans hum a soothing tune,
As layers set 'neath the glowing moon,
And slicers deftly slice and dice,
Turning visions into prints precise.

But wait, what's this, a clog, a glitch?
Nozzle woes, oh, what a stitch!
But fear not, for in our stash,
Are spare nozzles, ready to dash.

In the kingdom of 3-D delight,
Where creativity takes flight,
Tools and gadgets, oh so witty,
Crafting marvels for our city!

So raise your filaments high and proud,
Let's toast to printing, long and loud,
For in this world of plastic dreams,
The possibilities gleam, or so it seems!

My comments:

The quality of the poem, the rhyming, and the technical correctness of
the issues was quite impressive. Chat definitely met the challenge!

MY INPUT: The wonderful world of TV streaming services

Identify 20 items about streaming services such as Disney+, MGM plus, Hulu and several more and the difficulties getting them set up and the difficulties using three remotes to find them and many other conflicting difficulties. Cover the difficulties finding programs you want to see like PBS programs and action movies. Please use specifics.

ChatGPT output:

Certainly! Here are 20 items related to streaming services and the associated difficulties:

Disney+ subscription

MGM streaming subscription

Hulu subscription

Netflix subscription

Amazon Prime Video subscription

Apple TV+ subscription

HBO Max subscription

Peacock subscription

Paramount+ subscription

Discovery+ subscription

ESPN+ subscription

YouTube TV subscription

Roku device for streaming

Amazon Fire TV Stick for streaming

Apple TV device for streaming

Smart TV with built-in streaming apps

Chromecast for streaming

Difficulties setting up multiple streaming accounts and remembering login information for each.

Confusion and frustration with using multiple remotes to navigate between different streaming apps on various devices.

Difficulty finding specific programs across different streaming platforms, such as PBS documentaries or action movies, leading to a time-consuming search process.

My comments:

Wonderful and complete list.

MY INPUT: TV streaming services

Please write a humorous story about all the above.

ChatGPT output:

Once upon a time in the chaotic realm of Couch Potato Kingdom, there lived a streaming aficionado named Larry. Armed with a plethora of streaming subscriptions and enough remote controls to launch a space mission, Larry embarked on a quest for the ultimate binge-watching experience.

Larry's journey began with the daunting task of setting up his arsenal of streaming services. Armed with his trusty laptop and a bottomless cup of coffee, he dove headfirst into the labyrinth of subscription options, creating an intricate web of passwords that even the most seasoned hacker would struggle to decipher.

But just as Larry thought he had conquered the digital jungle; he encountered his first foe: the dreaded multiple remotes dilemma. With one remote for Disney+, another for Hulu, and yet another for Netflix, Larry found himself juggling more gadgets than a circus performer on a tightrope.

As he attempted to navigate between streaming apps, Larry's living room resembled a battlefield, with remotes flying through the air like missiles and frantic button mashing echoing through the air. "Where's the darn HBO Max button?" he exclaimed, his frustration reaching new heights.

But just when Larry thought things couldn't get any crazier, he stumbled upon the ultimate challenge: finding the perfect program to watch across his myriad of streaming platforms. With a hankering for PBS documentaries and a craving for action-packed movies, Larry embarked on a wild goose chase through the digital wilderness.

Hours turned into days as Larry sifted through endless menus and recommendation algorithms, encountering everything from historical dramas to cooking shows featuring celebrity chefs with questionable taste in aprons. "Surely, there must be an easier way to find something to watch!" he cried, his patience wearing thin.

But just as Larry was about to throw in the towel and return to the good old days of cable TV, a stroke of luck descended upon him. With a click of a button (or maybe it was two buttons... or three?), Larry stumbled upon the perfect program—a thrilling action movie followed by a riveting PBS documentary about the history of cheese.

And so, with a satisfied grin and a newfound appreciation for the absurdities of modern entertainment, Larry settled back into his throne (aka the couch) and prepared for a binge-watching marathon of epic proportions. For in the wacky world of streaming services, every mishap and misadventure only adds to the hilarity of the journey.

My comments:

I 'm not sure the phrase, "With one remote for Disney+, another for Hulu, and yet another for Netflix" is really true. Chat could have focused more on navigating on-screen choices rather than this strong emphasis on remotes. On screen choices are hard enough to decipher. Overall, it was quite good.

MY INPUT: **Ordering at a restaurant**

Write a story about four fussy dinners each with particular requests such as ultra-sensitive dietary restrictions focusing on low carbs and more veggies, low salt requirements, exact level of meat doneness, and the selecting the precise wine for the dinner.

ChatGPT output:

Fine Dining Follies: A Tale of Four Diners

In the realm of haute cuisine, where culinary masterpieces are served on plates the size of postage stamps and the wine list reads like a Shakespearean epic, there exists a particular breed of diner. They are the meticulous, the particular, the ones who turn the simple act of ordering a meal into an Olympic-level event. Join me now as we delve into the uproarious world of four such individuals, each with their own quirks and idiosyncrasies, as they navigate the treacherous waters of a fancy upscale restaurant.

Our story begins with Patricia, a woman with a laundry list of dietary restrictions that could rival the tax code in complexity. As she peruses the menu with the intensity of a detective on a case, her eyes scan for the elusive combination of no carbs and copious vegetables. Finally, she settles on a dish, but not without a barrage of substitutions and alterations that would make even the most seasoned chef break out in a cold sweat. "No potatoes," she declares to the waiter, "replace them with espresso sprouts, add extra vegetables, and hold the sauce...actually, can you add a splash of balsamic reduction instead?"

Meanwhile, seated across from Patricia is Harold, whose aversion to salt rivals that of a slug on a salt flat. With a furrowed brow, he peppers the waiter with questions about the salt content of no fewer than seven dishes, each query more incredulous than the last. "Are you sure there's no salt in the risotto? What about the sea bass? Can you check with the chef to make sure there's absolutely no salt whatsoever?"

Next to Harold sits Gerald, a man who takes his red meat very seriously indeed. As he debates with the waiter the optimal temperature for his steak, the kitchen resembles a battleground, with chefs locked in a heated debate over the merits of medium-well versus well-done. "That's a touch too high a temperature for my liking," Gerald remarks with a frown, "perhaps we could lower it a notch or two? I don't want to risk any undue charring."

Lastly, we have Veronica, the resident wine aficionado whose knowledge rivals that of a sommelier. With a flourish, she interrogates the waiter about the vintage year, the terroir, and the subtle nuances of each bottle on the extensive wine list. "Was it a rainy year in Napa? Did the grapes express notes of chocolate and peanuts, with just a hint of smokiness? And what about the French wine? Was it a sunny vintage in Burgundy, or did the clouds roll in at just the right moment?"

As the meal progresses, so too does the chaos, culminating in a cacophonous symphony of clinking glasses and raised voices as the check arrives. Armed with calculators and a determination bordering on madness, the four diners engage in a fierce battle of mathematics, each one arguing vehemently for their share of the bill. But in the end, after much deliberation and a few choice words exchanged, they reach a truce, united in their quest for fairness and equity.

And so, dear reader, as the curtain falls on our culinary comedy of requests, we bid farewell to Patricia, Harold, Gerald, and Veronica, each with their own quirks and foibles, but united in their love of fine dining and the occasional spat over the bill. Until next time, bon appétit!

My comments:

The detail was quite enjoyable, but there is a subtle logical and contextual mix-up in the conversation about the temperature of the steak. Chat suddenly skips from Gerald talking to the waiter to Gerald talking to the chef. Gerald would not have been in the kitchen!

MY INPUT: **A trip through TSA at the airport**

A trip through TSA at the airport (Note: this is a second story about the TSA as I find it the worst part of a trip and the most stressful, so I wanted to emphasize it.)

Write a humorous story about all the difficulties of going through TSA at the airport. Include taking your laptop out, your phones, your belt, making sure your pants don't fall down, then waiting forever for your bag to come out of the x-ray and etc.

ChatGPT output:

Dave had traveled a lot for work, but nothing could prepare him for the circus act that was modern airport security. He approached the TSA checkpoint with the precision of a seasoned veteran, but even veterans have their off days.

First, the shoes. He had worn his trusty slip-ons, but somehow, today they decided to fight back. He pried them off with the grace of a drunken flamingo, nearly falling into the conveyor belt.

Next, the laptop. Of course, it was buried in the bottom of his bag. He swore it hadn't been this deep when he packed it. As he rummaged through socks, underwear, and what felt like the remnants of a high school science project, he finally found it. Triumphantly, he placed it in the bin, only to remember his phone.

"Please remove all electronics larger than a cell phone," the TSA officer droned. Dave glanced around nervously. He had three. Why? Because life without constant digital distraction was apparently too much to bear. He pulled out his work phone, his personal phone, and the mysterious third phone he swore he needed for "emergencies." All went into the bin.

Next came the belt. Dave had gained a few pounds since his last trip, and his belt was now not just an accessory but a necessity. As he unbuckled it, he could feel his pants starting to plot their escape. He tightened his core muscles and prayed gravity wouldn't betray him.

Finally, he was ready. He approached the scanner, hands raised in a gesture that felt more like surrender than compliance. The scanner beeped. The TSA agent gestured for him to step aside. Great, random screening, his favorite.

"Sir, please hold out your hands."

He did, feeling like a wizard about to cast a spell. The agent swabbed his palms, then fed the swab into a machine that looked like it belonged in a sci-fi movie. It beeped ominously. Dave's heart raced.

"It's just a false alarm, sir. Please proceed."

Dave walked back to the conveyor belt, where his belongings were still undergoing their own private drama. His laptop had somehow flipped itself over, and his phones were scattered like a digital Easter egg hunt. His shoes were on a separate conveyor belt altogether, heading towards what looked like a lost and found pile.

Then came the waiting. His bag had been flagged for further inspection. He watched as it was pulled aside, its contents scrutinized as if it held the secrets of the universe.

"Is this your bag, sir?" the TSA agent asked.

"Yes," Dave replied, trying to sound patient.

The agent pulled out a bottle of water.

"You can't bring this on the plane."

"Right, sorry," Dave mumbled, taking the offending item and chucking it into a bin that looked suspiciously like a black hole.

Finally, his bag was cleared. He gathered his belongings, balancing the laptop on one arm while slipping his shoes on with the other. His phones went back into various pockets, and he struggled to buckle his belt without setting everything down again. His pants, thankfully, stayed up.

Dave walked away from the TSA checkpoint feeling like he had just completed an obstacle course designed by sadistic clowns. As he headed towards his gate, he couldn't help but laugh at the absurdity of it all. Travel was supposed to be glamorous, but instead, it was a series of small, ridiculous battles. And somehow, that made the destination even sweeter.

My comments:

This story had delightful detail and I was happy to see chat included the requirement for further item inspection as this always introduces frustrating delays. There appeared to be some logic issue surrounding the pants. If Dave put on weight, shouldn't the pants be tighter and not at risk of escaping? In spite of the logic issue, chat created the amusing phrase, "As he unbuckled it, he could feel his pants starting to plot their escape."

Chat output: The delivery of the US mail (sometimes)

(an original case with no input shown)

It was a day like any other in our neighborhood, filled with the usual chaos and charm that comes with suburban living. But for us, the highlight of the day was always the arrival of the mail. Not because we were eagerly awaiting any particular letter or package, but because the sheer unpredictability of our mail delivery never failed to entertain.

You see, in our little corner of the world, mail delivery was an adventure in itself. It was like playing a game of roulette, except instead of a spinning wheel, we had a rotating cast of mailmen who seemed to operate on their own mysterious schedules.

Spotty mail delivery was the norm. Some days, our mail would arrive promptly at 3 o'clock in the afternoon, just as we were starting to wonder if it would ever show up. Other days, it would saunter in fashionably late, making its grand entrance at 7:45 in the evening, long after we'd given up hope.

But the real comedy began when the mail was actually delivered. Small packages, large packages, letters, bills – you name it, we got it. Or rather, we got some of it. Because more often than not, our mail was delivered to the wrong address.

We'd receive letters addressed to people who hadn't lived in our house for years – two years ago, five years ago, eleven years ago. Once, we even received a state of California disbursement check made out to someone we'd never heard of, probably worth a hefty sum of $2,500. It was like winning the lottery, except without the actual winnings.

And then there were our neighbors next door, who seemed to be in a perpetual state of mail-related confusion. Their mailbox was clearly marked "Hold and Do Not Deliver," but that didn't deter our mailman. Instead of holding their mail as instructed, he simply dumped it all into our mailbox, figuring it was close enough.

We became unwitting recipients of their mail, from bills to catalogs to what seemed like a never-ending stream of junk mail. It was like Christmas morning, except instead of presents, we got other people's overdue credit card statements.

But the real kicker was when we needed to sign for a package. If we weren't home, we'd find a scribbled note on our front door instructing us to pick up our mail at the post office. And so, we'd embark on the epic journey to the post office, braving long lines and surly clerks, all for the privilege of deciphering a signature that looked like it had been written by a particularly unruly chicken.

And of course, when we finally reached the front of the line (after waiting for the 19 people ahead of us) and presented our note, the clerk would inevitably inform us that she couldn't release the package without authorization from the postmaster. It was a Kafkaesque nightmare of bureaucratic red tape, all for a package that probably contained nothing more exciting than a pair of socks we'd ordered online.

But despite the chaos, the confusion, and the occasional frustration, there was a certain charm to our haphazard mail delivery system. It was like a daily dose of comic relief, a reminder that sometimes, life's little absurdities are the things that bring us the most joy. And so, we embraced the madness, secure in the knowledge that no matter what else might happen, at least we'd always have our mail – eventually.

My comments:

There was a subtle logical error related to signing the document at the post office. Instead of the person receiving the mail having to sign, chat somehow got confused and focused on "... deciphering a signature" ... an existing signature. Otherwise, this was an enjoyable list of frequently occurring mail delivery issues.

MY INPUT: Two old friends have coffee together

Special note: O. Henry was a famous short story writer who lived from 1862 to 1910 and wrote about the lives of people. He mainly wrote about people in New York. This vignette is not intended to be humorous but rather to illustrate the versatility of chat.

Write a story in the style of O. Henry about two old friends who go to the coffee shop in the morning and enjoy the conversation.

ChatGPT output:

In the heart of a bustling city, nestled between towering buildings and bustling streets, stood a quaint little coffee shop named "Evelyn's Brew." Every morning, like clockwork, two old friends, Harold and Arthur, shuffled through its doors, their laughter echoing amidst the aroma of freshly brewed coffee.

Harold, with his unruly shock of white hair and twinkling blue eyes, always arrived first, settling into his favorite corner booth. Arthur, a bit more stooped but with a mischievous glint in his gray eyes, joined him shortly after, carrying with him the day's newspaper.

Their friendship had weathered decades, surviving the trials of time like an ancient oak enduring the fiercest storms. They met in their youth, a pair of dreamers with nothing but the world stretched out before them. Through the highs and lows of life, they remained constants in each other's ever-changing landscapes.

As they sipped their steaming cups of coffee, Harold regaled Arthur with tales of his latest adventures, exaggerated for effect but always captivating. Arthur would nod along, occasionally interjecting with a witty remark or a well-timed joke, the lines on his face deepening with laughter.

But amidst the banter and camaraderie, there lingered a bittersweet undertone. Time had woven threads of silver into their hair and etched lines upon their faces, a reminder of the fleeting nature of life. They knew their days of shared laughter were numbered, and yet they savored each moment as if it were their last.

One chilly morning, as they sat huddled over their cups of coffee, Harold reached across the table, clasping Arthur's weathered hand in his own. "We've had a good run, old friend," he said, his voice tinged with nostalgia.

Arthur squeezed his hand in return, a silent acknowledgment passing between them. They had journeyed through life together, facing its joys and sorrows hand in hand. And though their steps had slowed, and their voices grown softer with age, their bond remained unbreakable, a testament to the enduring power of friendship.

As the sun rose higher in the sky, casting golden rays through the coffee shop windows, Harold and Arthur continued their conversation, their laughter ringing out like a melody in the morning air. For in each other's company, they found solace, strength, and the simple joy of shared moments that transcended the passage of time.

My comments:

This story truly illustrated the versatility of chat. It was a poignant and touching story that touched the lives of two men, their friendship, and the grace of aging. Way to go chat!

MY INPUT: Ordering drive through fast food with children

Write about ordering drive through fast food with the children (Louis and Olivia). Be sure to add some ordering conflict.

ChatGPT Output:

Fast Food Follies

It was a sunny day, and the family car rolled up to Jack-in-the-Box with Louis and Olivia in the back seat, their stomachs growling like a pack of hungry wolves.

Olivia, the pint-sized dictator of the menu, wasted no time in declaring her demands. "Fries!" she shouted, her voice echoing through the car like a tiny but mighty megaphone.

But mom armed with nutritional wisdom, stood her ground. "Fries aren't the best choice, Olivia. They are not good for you. How about a burger with cheese instead?"

Olivia's response was a resounding "No!" followed by a chorus of "I want fries! Daddy lets me have fries!"

Meanwhile, Louis, the sauce aficionado, had his own battle to wage. "Ranch! Barbecue! Green goddess! Italian!" he exclaimed, listing off sauces like a seasoned sommelier presenting a fine wine selection.

But alas, the drive-through gods were not feeling particularly accommodating that day. "You'll have to pick just one sauce, Louis," mom explained, hoping to quell the impending sauce storm.

"Why do I have to pick just one?" Louis whined; his disappointment palpable.

Olivia ordered two milk shakes and a Diet Coke. Mom said no! In a stroke of genius (or perhaps madness), Olivia revealed her secret weapon: "Daddy lets me order two milkshakes!"

With the chaos reaching its peak, mom made a tactical retreat, opting for the tried-and-true "Daddy Maneuver" of circling Jack-in-the-box back to the drive thru for a second round of ordering.

Eventually, the orders were placed, albeit with a few compromises along the way. Olivia got her burger and fries and only one milk shake (because who can resist the power of a determined child?), Louis settled on a single sauce (albeit begrudgingly).

Sure enough, as they pulled away from the window, Olivia's voice pierced the air like a siren. "You forgot my Diet Coke!"

Mom sighed, resigned to her fate. "Straight to the psych ward," she muttered under her breath, as she navigated the chaos of the drive-through and the even greater chaos of parenthood.

And so, with their fast-food feast in hand and their sanity hanging by a thread, the family car drove off into the sunset, ready to face whatever culinary adventures awaited them next. After all, in the world of fast food and family, there's never a dull moment—especially when Louis and Olivia are involved.

As mom, tired and highly frustrated, drove into her driveway with the back seat covered with sticky sauce and spilled milkshake, she smiled to herself and thought, "there's a certain appeal to the psych ward." After calming down, mom had a better thought, "maybe a day at a luxurious spa would be better than the psych ward."

My comments:

I added the last the last two sentences to enhance the humor. I couldn't resist as I have seen my friend's car with spilled milkshake and sticky sauce on the back seat and on the floor. There is no way you can keep a car completely clean when you order food from a drive through with children! Chat truly captured the complexity and frustration of ordering with children.

MY INPUT: **The difficulty of using the web**

Write a humorous story, emphasizing the frustrating emotion of navigating websites. Include such items as the difficulty signing on and then finding out that after you enter your email it says that that email is already being used and gives you no indication how to resolve the problem. Also talk about the frustration experience after filling out six lines of information and then having the website say you can't proceed because something was erroneously missing but doesn't tell you what to do to fix the problem. Also, write about the frustration of trying to find the red continue button, which is hiding way down at the end of four pages you must scroll through. Why can't they put the continue button near where you're entering the data? And then, of course, add a bit about a 40% discount if you order in the next two minutes. For sure, the descriptions are so poor you can't find out what you want in the next two minutes. Then finally conclude with some kind of surprise ending.

ChatGPT output:

Once upon a time, in the vast and treacherous realm of the internet, there existed a website so confounding, so labyrinthine, that it could only be described as a digital dungeon of despair. This was the tale of Bob, a brave soul who dared to venture into the depths of this virtual maze in search of a simple purchase.

Bob, armed with his trusty mouse and a cup of coffee to fuel his courage, approached the website with cautious optimism. Little did he know, he was about to embark on an odyssey fraught with frustration.

His journey began innocuously enough, as he attempted to sign in. But alas, the website had other plans. After entering his email address, he was met with a cruel message: "Email already in use." No guidance, no solution, just a digital dead end.

Undeterred, Bob forged ahead, determined to conquer this digital beast. He diligently filled out six lines of information, only to be met with another obstacle: an error message claiming something was missing. What that something was, the website refused to divulge, leaving Bob stranded in a sea of confusion.

But Bob was not one to give up easily. With steely resolve, he scoured the screen for the elusive continue button, which seemed to be playing a game of hide-and-seek amidst the endless pages of forms. "Why can't they put it near where you're entering the data?" Bob muttered to himself, frustration bubbling beneath the surface.

Just as he was about to throw in the towel, a glimmer of hope appeared in the form of a pop-up window. "Act now and receive a 40% discount if you order in the next two minutes!" it proclaimed. Excited at the prospect of saving some coin, Bob clicked eagerly, only to be greeted by a barrage of poorly written descriptions and confusing options. Two minutes passed in the blink of an eye, and Bob was left empty-handed once more.

But just when it seemed like all hope was lost, a miracle occurred. In a moment of clarity, Bob noticed a small, inconspicuous link hidden at the bottom of the page: "Skip to checkout." With a mixture of relief and disbelief, Bob clicked the link and was whisked away to the promised land of purchasing simplicity.

And so, dear reader, let this be a cautionary tale for all who dare to venture into the tangled web of online shopping. For amidst the chaos and confusion, there may yet be a glimmer of hope waiting to guide you to your destination. Just remember to keep your wits about you, and perhaps, just perhaps, you'll emerge victorious in the end.

My comments:

Chat followed my input quite closely. Somehow, I expected chat to add some troublesome web navigation experiences of its own. A minor point, web sites usually say to click a "button" to proceed to checkout, and not to click a "link", which is usually a URL. All in all, chat did an impressive job.

Chat output: Water Polo

(an original case with no input shown)

Once upon a time, in the bustling halls of Ridgemont High, there were two towering figures who ruled the school with a mix of athleticism and unexpected intellect.

First, there was Madison, a blonde with a wingspan that could rival a condor's. She was the star of the water polo team, fighting through the pool like a high power dedicated athlete. But Madison wasn't just brawn; she was also a brainiac, acing every test without breaking a sweat, much to the disbelief of her classmates who thought being tall and blonde automatically meant she was all brawn and no brain.

Then, there was Jake, the lanky basketball prodigy with a wingspan that made him a defensive nightmare for opponents. He could dunk with the finesse of a ballet dancer and shoot three-pointers with the precision of a surgeon. But Jake wasn't just a jock; he had a wit as sharp as his jump shot, often leaving his teammates and teachers in stitches with his off-the-cuff remarks.

Despite their differences, Madison and Jake shared a unique bond that transcended their respective sports. They were like two peas in a pod, albeit two very tall peas. They would often be spotted in the library, heads bent over textbooks, arguing passionately about everything from quantum physics to the latest sports scandals.

Their friendship was the stuff of legend at Ridgemont High, but it wasn't without its fair share of comedic mishaps. Like the time Madison accidentally dunked her biology textbook into the pool during practice, resulting in a soggy mess of DNA diagrams and waterlogged pages. Or when Jake tried to impress Madison by reciting Shakespearean sonnets during halftime, only to trip over his own shoelaces and face-plant onto the court.

But through it all, Madison and Jake laughed off their misadventures, knowing that they were better together than apart. And as they navigated the ups and downs of high school life, they proved that being tall, blonde, and athletically gifted didn't mean you couldn't also be smart, funny, and absolutely unforgettable.

My comments:

Impressive job of describing the student/athlete and breaking the stereotype of athletes not being excellent students.

MY INPUT: **The frustrations of golf**

Write a humorous, satirical article on golf and the problems and frustrations of golf

ChatGPT output:

"Swinging in Circles: The Comical Chaos of Golf"

In a world where grown adults willingly chase a tiny white ball around meticulously landscaped lawns, the sport of golf has managed to maintain its status as the pinnacle of refined leisure – or so they say. Behind the facade of perfectly manicured greens and polite applause lies a world riddled with absurdities and frustrations that would make even the most patient individual question their sanity.

Firstly, let's talk about the wardrobe. Golf attire seems to be stuck in a time warp, with players donning attire that wouldn't look out of place in a 1950s country club. Who decided that pastel-colored polos and pants that could double as sails were the epitome of fashion? And don't even get me started on the ubiquitous plaid pants that seem to have been salvaged from the set of a retro sitcom.

Then there's the equipment – a baffling array of clubs designed to hit a ball into a tiny hole hundreds of yards away. Each club comes with its own obscure name and purpose, leaving newcomers to the sport scratching their heads in confusion. Who knew that choosing the right club could be akin to selecting a wand in Harry Potter?

And let's not forget the actual gameplay – a delicate dance of precision and frustration. Despite hours of practice and thousands of dollars spent on lessons, the average golfer still manages to slice, hook, and shank their way around the course with all the grace of a drunken giraffe on roller skates. It's a sport where the ball somehow always ends up in the most inconvenient of places – behind trees, in sand traps, or nestled snugly in the rough.

But perhaps the greatest source of amusement in the world of golf is the culture that surrounds it. From the obligatory post-round drink at the clubhouse to the endless debates over handicaps and rules, golfers seem to revel in their own peculiar brand of masochism. After all, what other sport encourages its participants to voluntarily spend hours traipsing through fields in search of a tiny, elusive object?

Despite its many quirks and frustrations, there's something undeniably addictive about the game of golf. Maybe it's the thrill of sinking that perfect putt or the camaraderie shared with fellow sufferers. Or perhaps it's simply the knowledge that no matter how bad things get on the course, there's always the promise of a cold drink and a good laugh waiting at the 19th hole.

So the next time you find yourself cursing at a stubborn divot or wrestling with a misbehaving putter, just remember – you're not alone. Welcome to the wacky world of golf, where the only thing more absurd than the sport itself is the people who play it.

My comments:

Chat is obviously quite familiar with the game of golf. I thought it was quite ingenious that chat came up with the phrase, "with all the grace of a drunken giraffe on roller skates."

MY INPUT: **Tennis anyone?**

Write a humorous satire about the game of tennis. Include a server who double faults, balls that land on the line and players who argue is it in or out, overly aggressive players who run up to the net, mostly for show. Discuss flashy, colorful tennis outfits with at least six logos all over the outfit. And, of course, cover fashionable water bottles and outrageous, colorful towels to refresh after the game.

ChatGPT output:

In the zany world of tennis, where the court is a battleground and the players are warriors armed with rackets, there exists a spectacle that transcends mere sport. Welcome to the Theatre of Double Faults, where the line between victory and defeat is as thin as a sliced backhand.

Picture, if you will, a server stepping up to the baseline, ready to unleash a thunderous serve that could split atoms. But alas, the gods of tennis have other plans as the ball is sent spiraling into the net, much to the dismay of the server and the amusement of the spectators. Double fault! Cue the awkward shuffle and the sheepish grin as the server contemplates the mysteries of life, like why their serve decided to take a detour to the bottom of the net.

Meanwhile, amidst the chaos of the game, a ball lands precariously on the line. Is it in? Is it out? Cue the dramatic slow-motion replays and the heated arguments between players, each one convinced that their perception of reality is the correct one. It's a battle of egos disguised as a debate over a few millimeters of turf.

But let's not forget the pièce de résistance – the players themselves, bedecked in their flashy, colorful outfits that could rival a peacock's plumage. Logos upon logos plastered all over their attire like battle scars from sponsors vying for attention. It's a fashion show masquerading as a sporting event, with each player trying to outdo the other in a game of sartorial one-upmanship.

And what would a tennis match be without the obligatory display of aggression? Players charging up to the net like knights on horseback, only to retreat at the first sign of trouble. It's all for show, of course, a carefully choreographed dance designed to intimidate opponents and entertain the crowds.

As the match reaches its climax, the players reach for their fashionable water bottles, emblazoned with logos of hydration and vitality. Each sip a statement, each gulp a declaration of superiority. And let's not forget the outrageous, colorful towels, wielded like flags of victory as players dab at their brows and refresh themselves after the grueling battle.

Yes, tennis is more than just a game. It's a spectacle, a circus of absurdity where the lines between sport and theater blur and the only thing that truly matters is the roar of the crowd and the thrill of the game. So let us raise our rackets high and salute the madness that is tennis, for where else can you find such a delightful combination of skill, style, and sheer unadulterated chaos?

My comments:

This was an ideal chat output. I created the instructions packed with specific humorous guidance and chat rose to the occasion. A minor point, chat created a plural for the word "double" as in, "Welcome to the Theatre of Doubles Faults." It had to be corrected.

Write a humorous story about a coffee shop experience. Talk about barista blunders where the barista makes mistakes and creates the wrong kind of coffee, talk about the drama of spilled coffee, talk about the sweet symphony of overheard conversations, talk about creative drink names such as the Unicorn Fappuccino, talk about getting work done over coffee including a woman who's on a zoom call discussing her department's $60,000 budget oblivious to amused glances of nearby patrons, talk about a lone figure immersed in a digital whirlwind surrounded by three screens— a laptop, an iPad, and an iPhone all vying for attention, talk about a young couple in love, hand in hand gazing adoringly into each other's eyes, and talk about a resident maestro, tapping his foot and swaying to the rhythm of a private concert played through his over oversized headphones and then wrap it up with some kind of humorous summary and an invitation to frequently visit your local coffee shop to observe the caffeinated circus.

ChatGPT output:

Caffeinated Chaos: A Day in the Life of Brewtopia

Welcome to Brewtopia, the quirkiest coffee shop in town, where every visit is a blend of aromatic adventures and unexpected amusements.

This particular morning started like any other, with our resident barista, Jake, already causing a stir. Known for his artistic flair and creative concoctions, today Jake decided to take it up a notch—or rather, several notches too many.

"One Unicorn Fappuccino coming up!" he declared, holding up a rainbow-colored drink topped with glittery whipped cream and sprinkles. The customer, expecting a plain black coffee, stared in disbelief. "Uh, I asked for a black coffee," she said, pointing to the psychedelic beverage. Jake blinked, then grinned sheepishly. "My bad! Guess I got carried away."

Next came the drama of the spilled coffee. A young man, engrossed in his phone, didn't see the puddle forming around his cup until it was too late. With a loud "Yikes!" and a spectacular flail, he managed to knock over not just his drink but also the adjacent sugar dispenser. Coffee and sugar cascaded across the counter, creating a sticky mess and prompting a collective gasp from the onlookers.

Meanwhile, the sweet symphony of overheard conversations filled the air. At one table, an animated discussion about a hamster's escape plan was in full swing. At another, a heated debate over the merits of pineapple on pizza (spoiler: no one won).

Amidst the chatter, a woman on a Zoom call could be heard discussing her department's $60,000 budget. She was oblivious to the amused glances of nearby patrons as she emphasized the need for "strategic allocation of funds." The irony of such serious talk in the whimsical environment of Brewtopia was not lost on anyone.

In one corner, a lone figure was immersed in a digital whirlwind, surrounded by three screens—a laptop, an iPad, and an iPhone—all vying for attention. The multitasking maestro was a sight to behold, his fingers dancing across keyboards while notifications pinged incessantly.

At the table by the window, a young couple sat hand in hand, gazing adoringly into each other's eyes. They were the picture of romance, their coffees forgotten in the glow of their affection. Their whispered sweet nothings added a touch of magic to the bustling shop.

And then there was the resident maestro, a regular at Brewtopia. He sat in his usual spot, tapping his foot and swaying to the rhythm of a private concert played through his oversized headphones. Occasionally, he would burst into an off-key rendition of whatever song he was listening to, much to the delight of those around him.

As the day wound down, the regulars trickled out, leaving behind the remnants of their caffeinated chaos. Jake, wiping down the counter, couldn't help but chuckle at the day's events. "Another day, another adventure," he mused.

So, if you ever find yourself in need of a good laugh, a dose of human drama, or just a spectacularly strange coffee, head on over to Brewtopia. It's the caffeinated circus you never knew you needed.

Come for the coffee, stay for the show!

My comments:

This output was cheerful, lighthearted, realistic and it flowed. I would definitely give it an "A". I'am not sure of the expression, "My bad! Guess I got carried away." Maybe "my bad" is an expression I am just unfamiliar with or an error. In the real world, I actually shared the table with the pleasant woman who was discussing her department budget while I was working on this book. She didn't care, I didn't care. The final sentence (Come for the coffee, stay for the show!) was, arguably, near genius!

For the input, I heavily borrowed several phrases from a previous chat output that I had rejected.

MY INPUT: What are the seven funniest aspects of cricket?

ChatGPT output:

Cricket, like baseball, has its fair share of quirks and amusing features that make it a beloved sport around the world. Here are seven of the funniest aspects of cricket:

1. **Unusual terminology**: Cricket has a plethora of terms that can sound downright bizarre to the uninitiated. From "googly" to "silly mid-off" and "slog sweep," the vocabulary of cricket is a treasure trove of comedic potential.

2. **Tea breaks**: Unlike most sports, cricket pauses for a formal tea break during longer matches. It's a quaint tradition that adds a touch of British charm to the game and leaves spectators wondering if the players are discussing strategy or debating the merits of Earl Grey vs. English Breakfast.

3. **Dress code**: Cricket players often sport white uniforms, which can lead to some hilarious moments when the action takes a messy turn. Nothing says comedy like a pristine white outfit covered in grass stains and mud.

4. **Fielding positions**: Cricket fielding positions have some delightfully absurd names, such as "silly mid-on," "backward square leg," and "long stop." Trying to decipher where each player is positioned can feel like playing a game of Twister with a map of the field.

5. **The Duckworth-Lewis method**: Named after statisticians Frank Duckworth and Tony Lewis, this method is used to calculate the target score for the team batting second in rain-affected matches. It's as confusing as it sounds and often leaves fans scratching their heads in bewilderment.

6. **Sledging**: Cricket is known for its tradition of sledging, where players engage in witty banter and psychological warfare to distract

their opponents. Some of the insults hurled on the field are so creative that they could rival the best stand-up comedy routines.

7. **Bizarre dismissals**: Cricket boasts a wide array of ways for batsmen to get out, including some truly bizarre methods such as being "hit wicket" (knocking over their own stumps), "handled the ball" (touching the ball with a hand not holding the bat), or being "obstructed the field" (interfering with a fielder). These unusual dismissals add an element of unpredictability and comedy to the game.

So there you have it, cricket's quirky and amusing side. Whether it's the peculiar terminology, the genteel tea breaks, or the inventive insults, cricket never fails to entertain both die-hard fans and casual spectators alike.

My comments:

Nice list that is probably quite unfamiliar to most readers. Whoever heard of the Ductwork- Lewis statistical method being part of a sports game? However, I enjoyed the strange terminology.

MY INPUT: Write a comedy piece about the above terms from cricket

ChatGPT output:

"Lost in Translation: A Comedy of Cricket Terms"

Scene: A cricket match is in full swing, with players scattered across the field in their crisp white uniforms. Amidst the action, two bewildered spectators, Bob and Sally, try to make sense of the bizarre terminology flying around them.

Bob: (scratching his head) What in the world is a "googly" supposed to be?

Sally: (squinting at the field) Beats me. Maybe it's some sort of dance move they do between overs.

Bob: (chuckling) Wouldn't surprise me. And what about "silly mid-off"? Are they mocking the fielder or just stating the obvious?

Sally: (pointing) Look, there's someone standing at "backward square leg." Is that like the Bermuda Triangle of cricket positions?

Bob: (nodding) And don't forget "long stop" over there. Is he guarding against runaway cricket balls or trying to catch the last train out of here?

Sally: (laughing) I have no idea, but I think I'd feel safer standing behind the "short leg" instead.

Bob: (spotting a player) Uh-oh, looks like someone's about to face a "googly." Quick, get ready to do the googly dance!

Sally: (joining in) Googly, googly, shake it all about! Hey, if it distracts the batsman, it's worth a shot!

As the match continues, Bob and Sally find themselves caught up in the absurdity of cricket terminology, turning each confusing term into an opportunity for comedic interpretation. From "slog sweep" to "silly mid-on," they embrace the madness of the game and revel in the joy of not taking it too seriously.

In the world of cricket, where the rules are as complex as the English countryside, Bob and Sally discover that laughter is the best way to navigate the maze of terminology and enjoy the timeless spectacle unfolding before them. And so, armed with humor and a healthy dose of confusion, they cheer on their favorite team, one googly dance at a time.

My comments:

Wonderful vocabulary. It's all Greek to me but it appears to be humorous Greek.

MY INPUT: Trip to the ER

Write a humorous article about a hospital ER with focus on the waiting room and getting into the ER. You come in and you see the first nurse and they do some minor triage and then you talk to another nurse for major triage. You wait and wait and then you get called back to answer a few more questions, and finally you get admitted where, if you're lucky, they have a room but usually the ER is busy and they put you in the hallway. Then you get an admin person to take your insurance or Medicare cards. Then finally you see a nurse who takes some additional information and maybe some blood and finally you see a doctor for 32 seconds.

ChatGPT output:

"Adventures in the ER: A Comedy of Waiting"

Welcome to the wild world of the hospital emergency room, where time moves slower than a snail on a coffee break and patience is more than just a virtue—it's a survival skill. Strap in and get ready for a hilarious journey through the chaos and confusion of the ER waiting room.

Scene 1: The Waiting Room You enter the ER, hoping for swift medical attention. Instead, you're greeted by a sea of anxious faces and the distant sound of coughing and sneezing. You approach the first nurse, who gives you a sympathetic smile and asks for your name, date of birth, and the reason for your visit. You comply, only to be directed to the waiting area, where you're left to ponder life's mysteries alongside a guy with a sprained ankle and a woman clutching a tissue box like it's her lifeline.

Scene 2: The Minor Triage After what feels like an eternity, you're finally summoned by another nurse for minor triage. You repeat your name and date of birth for the umpteenth time and answer a barrage of questions about your medical history, symptoms, and whether or not you've recently traveled to Mars. You're assured that someone will be with you shortly and ushered back to the waiting room, where time seems to stand still.

Scene 3: The Major Triage Just when you've resigned yourself to spending the rest of your days in the waiting room, you're called back again, this time for major triage. You answer even more questions, wondering if the nurse is secretly auditioning for Jeopardy. Then, just when you think you've covered every possible topic known to mankind, you're informed that the doctor will be with you shortly. Spoiler alert: "shortly" is a relative term in the ER.

Scene 4: Admission, or Lack Thereof Finally, you're admitted to the inner sanctum of the ER, where an administrative person takes your Medicare or insurance cards with the efficiency of a seasoned card shark. You're handed a "stylish" hospital gown and shown to your "room," which is really just a spot in the hallway next to a vending machine and a screaming child. Ah, the lap of luxury. Oh, let's not forget the insertion of the IV. First the nurse has to find the proper blood vessel which usually takes five to seven painful stabs, and then finally inserts the primary needle that feels like a 1/4-inch rod. Then they wrap it all up and tape it and tell you don't ever move your arm, don't ever go to the bathroom, don't ever breathe heavily!

Scene 5: The Nurse's Interrogation A nurse swoops in to take your vital signs again and asks yet more questions about your medical history, allergies, and whether or not you prefer cats or dogs. You're starting to wonder if they're just stalling for time, but before you can voice your suspicions, they're off to tend to the next patient, leaving you to contemplate the mysteries of the universe once again.

Scene 6: The Lightning Round with the Doctor Finally, after what feels like an eternity, you're graced with the presence of the doctor. They breeze in, ask a few perfunctory questions, maybe take some blood if you're lucky, and then disappear faster than a magician's assistant. Before you know it, you're being ushered out the door with a handful of prescriptions, an MRI and a CT scan order (the scans will actually happen six hours later) and a vague sense of bewilderment.

Conclusion: And there you have it, folks: a whirlwind tour of the ER, where waiting is the name of the game and patience is your greatest weapon. So next time you find yourself in the emergency room, just remember to pack a good book, a snack, and a healthy dose of humor—because in the end, laughter truly is the best medicine.

PS: And for all this your insurance company gets billed for $29,599.

My comments:

Having been in the ER several times myself, I couldn't help editing in the $29,599 and the IV, MRI and CT orders. The phrase, ". . . asks yet more questions about your medical history, allergies, and whether or not you prefer cats or dogs" was enjoyable. Chat did add significant humor to each scene.

MY INPUT: What are the seven most useful features of ChatGPT?

Special note: this is the second story related to chat's capabilities. The first asked for "aspects" of chat and this one asked for "features" of chat. I included two stories because getting to know the strength of chat is so important.

ChatGPT output:

ChatGPT offers a wide array of features that can be incredibly useful across different contexts. Here are seven of the most useful features:

1. **Natural Language Understanding and Generation:**
   o ChatGPT excels at understanding and generating human-like text. This makes it useful for drafting emails, writing essays, creating content, and engaging in natural-sounding conversations.

2. **Personalized Assistance:**
   o The ability to remember context and preferences allows ChatGPT to provide more personalized responses. This can help in tailoring recommendations, remembering user details across sessions, and providing customized support.

3. **Information Retrieval:**
   o ChatGPT can quickly provide information on a wide range of topics, from historical facts to current events, making it a valuable resource for quick reference and learning.

4. **Multilingual Support:**
   o It can understand and generate text in multiple languages, enabling users from different linguistic backgrounds to interact with it and get assistance in their preferred language.

5. **Problem Solving:**
   - o Whether it's solving math problems, providing coding assistance, or helping with logical puzzles, ChatGPT can assist with a variety of problem-solving tasks.

6. **Creative Assistance:**
   - o ChatGPT can help with creative tasks such as brainstorming ideas, writing stories or poems, and even generating artwork concepts. It can be a valuable tool for artists, writers, and creative professionals.

7. **Conversational Practice:**
   - o For those learning a new language or looking to improve their conversational skills, ChatGPT can serve as a practice partner, providing a safe and responsive environment to practice speaking and writing.

These features make ChatGPT a versatile and powerful tool for both personal and professional use.

My comments:

This is definitely an impressive list.

MY INPUT: Write a humorous story using the previous useful features of chat

ChatGPT output:

Once upon a time in a small village called Bitburg, there lived a quirky inventor named Sam. Sam was known for creating strange gadgets and gizmos that often had minds of their own. One day, Sam stumbled upon an old, dusty book that described a magical artifact called the "ChatGPT Crystal." Intrigued by its promise of unparalleled assistance, Sam decided to find it.

After weeks of searching, Sam discovered the crystal in a hidden cave. To his surprise, it began to glow and speak:

"Greetings, Sam! I am the ChatGPT Crystal, your ultimate helper. How may I assist you today?"

Sam, being an inventor, immediately had a thousand ideas. "Can you help me draft a letter to the mayor about installing new streetlights?" he asked.

The crystal responded, "Certainly! Here's a professional yet persuasive draft." Sam marveled at the crystal's natural language skills.

Next, Sam wanted to personalize his inventions for his friends. "Can you remember my friends' preferences and help me customize their gifts?"

"Of course," said the crystal. "Just tell me about them, and I'll keep track of their likes and dislikes."

Impressed, Sam then sought information for his latest project. "What can you tell me about solar power advancements in 2024?"

The crystal provided a comprehensive summary, including the latest breakthroughs and innovations.

"Wow, you know so much!" Sam exclaimed. "Can you help me translate this manual into Spanish for my friend, Luis?"

"¡Por supuesto!" the crystal replied, seamlessly translating the document.

With each passing day, Sam's projects became more ambitious. One day, he needed help solving a complex equation for his newest invention. "Can you solve this math problem for me?"

The crystal quickly provided the solution, much to Sam's delight.

Feeling creative, Sam then asked, "Can you help me brainstorm ideas for a new story about a time-traveling toaster?"

The crystal generated a wild plot involving a toaster that accidentally became a hero in various historical events. Sam couldn't stop laughing at the absurdity.

Finally, Sam realized the crystal's true potential. "Can you be my conversation partner? I want to improve my French."

"Bien sûr! Let's practice," the crystal replied, engaging Sam in lively conversations.

Days turned into weeks, and Sam's inventions, language skills, and creativity soared. One evening, Sam sat in his workshop, surrounded by his successful projects, and looked at the glowing crystal. "You know, ChatGPT Crystal, you're not just a tool. You're a friend."

The crystal sparkled brighter than ever. "And you, Sam, are an inspiration. Together, we can achieve anything."

And so, Sam and the ChatGPT Crystal continued their adventures, transforming Bitburg into a hub of innovation, laughter, and creativity. They proved that with the right tools and a bit of humor, even the quirkiest dreams could come true.

And they lived happily ever after, surrounded by glowing streetlights and time-traveling toasters. The end.

My comments:

The story accurately followed the seven most useful features. Funny thing, after reading the sentence "You know, ChatGPT Crystal, you're not just a tool. You're a friend" I realized that after spending months writing this book, I am beginning to get a "feel" for chat and possibly I have developed a quasi-friend-like feeling towards chat. In summary: chat is a "friend" and a talented writing assistant.

MY INPUT: A pleasant evening watching TV as a family

Write a humorous story about a family who wants to spend a special evening watching TV together. There's mom and dad and Megan age 12 and Sean age 6. Now they have to decide what to watch. There are many choices: a sitcom, a police action thriller, an action show with cars flipping over and flying through the air, a Hallmark romcom, an ordinary thriller, a PBS special, a murder mystery, an old I love Lucy on YouTube, an animated Disney movie, a house renovation on HGTV, a dating show, and finally a baking contest. So many choices! Mom just wants the family to experience something together, dad is torn between relaxing and action movies, Megan would like something right for her age and Sean would love to see cars on fire flying through the air or any other action show. What should they watch? Be sure to make it humorous.

ChatGPT output:

It was a quiet Saturday evening in the Johnson household, and the air buzzed with excitement. Tonight was no ordinary night; it was the first official Family TV Night in ages. As the clock struck 7 PM, Mom, Dad, Megan (age 12), and Sean (age 6) gathered in the living room, each armed with their favorite snacks. Mom, the heart of the family, was on a mission. "Let's pick something we can all enjoy together," she announced with a hopeful smile. Dad, leaning back in his recliner, muttered, "Yeah, as long as it's not another Hallmark movie. I've reached my quota of predictability for the year."

Megan rolled her eyes. "Ugh, Dad, Hallmark is totally basic. Besides, it's not even Christmas. "Sean, already bouncing with excitement, exclaimed, "I want to see cars explode and fly! Vroom vroom! Boom! "The remote control lay on the coffee table, a symbol of ultimate power. It was up to them to decide which show would grace their screen tonight. First up,

Mom suggested, "How about a nice sitcom? We can all use a good laugh. "Megan scrunched her nose. "Aren't those for old people? No offense, Dad. "Dad chuckled, "None taken. But I wouldn't mind a good police action thriller. Some high-speed chases, a bit of mystery."

Sean's eyes widened. "Will there be cars flying? "Mom sighed, "How about an animated Disney movie? Something light and fun." Sean groaned. "No princesses, please! I want action!" Megan piped up, "What about a baking contest show? Those are cool, and maybe we can bake something together afterward." Dad laughed, "Last time we baked together, the kitchen looked like a flour bomb exploded." Mom's face lit up. "What about a house renovation on HGTV? We could get ideas for our own place." Megan and Sean groaned in unison. "Boring!"

Mom tried again. "A PBS special? Something educational?" The collective groan from Dad, Megan, and Sean was louder than before. Megan had an idea. "How about an old I Love Lucy episode on YouTube? It's classic and funny." Dad perked up, "Now that's an idea. Lucy's antics never get old." Sean, still focused on his action dream, said, "But where are the explosions?" Megan shot back, "Lucy does have a knack for disaster, you know." Finally, Dad suggested, "How about an action show with cars flipping over and flying through the air?" Sean jumped up, "YES! Finally!" Mom looked worried. "But isn't that a bit too much for Sean?" Sean puffed out his chest. "I can handle it, Mom. I'm almost seven!"

After a heated debate that could rival a Senate floor argument, they decided to compromise. They'd start with an I Love Lucy episode to satisfy the nostalgia and humor, followed by an action-packed car-flipping show for Sean (and secretly Dad). As the screen lit up with Lucy's iconic antics, the family settled in, laughter filling the room. Even Sean was captivated by Lucy's slapstick comedy. And after Lucy's shenanigans ended, they geared up for some high-octane car action.

Mom looked around at her family, their faces lit up by the TV screen. She smiled, realizing that it didn't matter what they watched. What mattered was that they were together, sharing these moments, and creating memories that would last a lifetime. Even if those memories included cars flipping and flying through the air.

My comments:

Another superb output. It looks like chat is quite familiar with family dynamics. I was wondering how chat would rationalize all the different motivations but it finally came up with the idea of two shows (possibly making the evening late, but it was a good solution).

MY INPUT: **Humorous quotes from children**

Show me humorous quotes from children. Emphasize quotes that have a life lesson in them.

ChatGPT OUTPUT

1. "Why do grown-ups never ask me for advice? I've been alive for 8 whole years!" - Unknown
2. "If you don't like where you are, just move. You're not a tree." - Unknown
3. "If at first, you don't succeed, then skydiving definitely isn't for you." - Unknown
4. "Never trust a dog to watch your food." - Patrick, age 10
5. "When life gives you lemons, make apple juice and let the world wonder how you did it." - Unknown
6. "If you want a rainbow, you gotta put up with the rain... or you could just buy a sprinkler." - Unknown
7. "Why do parents get mad when I sleep during the day? Isn't that when the brain recharges?" - Unknown
8. "I'm not arguing, I'm just explaining why I'm right." - Unknown
9. "You can't make everybody happy. You're not pizza." – Unknown

My comments:

Actual chat response was about one second! I'm not sure the "skydiving" and the "I'm not arguing" quotes are from children as I have seen them passed around the internet several times.

MY INPUT: Lazy and relaxing

Write a new humorous, story using dillydallying, lollygagging, and sauntering, all human behaviors.

ChatGPT output:

Once upon a time in the bustling city of Urbania, there lived a trio of friends: Lily, Max, and Emily. Each had their own unique quirks, but they shared a common love for leisurely activities, often dillydallying, lollygagging, and sauntering their way through life.

One sunny Saturday morning, the three friends decided to embark on a quest to find the best ice cream parlor in town. Lily, the queen of dillydallying, insisted they take the scenic route, stopping to smell the flowers and admire the architecture along the way. Max, the king of lollygagging, couldn't resist pausing every few steps to check his phone or strike up a conversation with passing strangers. And Emily, the master of sauntering, glided gracefully down the sidewalk, taking in the sights with an air of effortless elegance.

As they meandered through the streets of Urbania, their stomachs growled in anticipation of the sweet treats that awaited them. But instead of hurrying to their destination, they took their time, indulging in the simple pleasures of their leisurely stroll.

Finally, after what seemed like an eternity of dillydallying, lollygagging, and sauntering, they arrived at the ice cream parlor. But to their dismay, there was a long line snaking out the door, filled with eager customers eager to satisfy their sweet cravings.

Undeterred, Lily, Max, and Emily joined the queue, their spirits undampened by the wait. As they waited patiently, they entertained themselves by dillydallying with the menu, lollygagging about their favorite flavors, and sauntering back and forth to stretch their legs.

Finally, after what felt like an eternity, they reached the front of the line and placed their orders. With cones in hand, they retreated to a nearby park to enjoy their hard-earned treats. And as they sat on a bench, basking in the warm sunshine, they couldn't help but laugh at the absurdity of their leisurely adventure.

For Lily, Max, and Emily, it wasn't just about the destination—it was about the journey. And as they savored every last lick of their ice cream, they knew that sometimes, the best things in life are worth dillydallying, lollygagging, and sauntering for.

My comments:

Chat quickly and accurately caught on to this slower pace of life that is so unusual in today's rush rush culture.

MY INPUT: **Southern expressions**

Find all the southern expressions you can like "we are standing in tall corn"

ChatGPT output

Sure, here are some southern expressions:

"Bless your heart" - often used to show sympathy or condescension.

"Well, butter my biscuit" - an exclamation of surprise or amazement.

"He's busy as a cat on a hot tin roof" - describes someone who is very busy or frantic.

"I'm fixin' to" - means "I'm about to" or "I intend to."

"She's sweeter than a Georgia peach" - a compliment to someone's sweetness or charm.

"He's got more nerve than a bum tooth" - describes someone who is bold or daring.

"Happier than a pig in mud" - describes extreme contentment or happiness.

"She's pretty as a magnolia in May" - a compliment to someone's beauty.

"I reckon" - means "I suppose" or "I guess."

"He's as stubborn as a mule" - describes someone who is very stubborn.

These are just a few examples, but there are many more colorful expressions in southern dialects.

MY INPUT:

Write a humorous, comical story, using the best seven of these southern expressions

ChatGPT output:

Once upon a time in a small southern town, there was a Rite Aid pharmacist named Miss Daisy Mae. She was as sweet as a Georgia peach and busier than a cat on a hot tin roof. One day, a gentleman walked into the store looking flustered and said, "Well, butter my biscuit, I've got a hankering for some relief!"

Miss Daisy Mae, with her charming southern drawl, replied, "Bless your heart, sugar, what seems to be the trouble?" The man explained he had a headache that felt like a mule kick and needed something stronger than a pot of coffee. Miss Daisy Mae chuckled, saying, "I reckon I've got just the thing for you!" She handed him a bottle of headache pills and said, "Take these, and you'll be happier than a pig in mud in no time!"

As the man left, he couldn't help but smile at Miss Daisy Mae's humor. He turned back and said, "You're as funny as a barrel of monkeys, Miss Daisy Mae!" She grinned and replied, "Well, thank you kindly! Y'all come back now, ya hear?"

And with that, the man left Rite Aid feeling lighter in both his head and his heart, grateful for Miss Daisy Mae's southern charm and her knack for fixing what ailed him.

My comments:

This refreshing Southern expression example is a case of preliminary chat output being used as an input to the main chat. Like other examples, I asked for a list of items, in this case, southern expressions, and then asked chat to write a story. Chat wrote the story in less than two seconds. Chat also created the list in less than two seconds. These Southern expressions are delightful.

MY INPUT: Aliens in Roswell, New Mexico

Write a humorous and comic article about the stories and myths concerning aliens landing in Roswell, New Mexico. Are they green with great big eyes? What did they look like? How long ago did the alleged aliens land in Roswell? Was it in the 1940s? Why did they land in the desert in Roswell, as opposed to forests in northern New York, for example. Now for the myth-breaking truth, which might be called the alleged truth. Who knows what the real truth is! In 1946 or 1947 the Army Air Corp was allegedly testing high altitude balloons for the purpose of detecting any kind of Soviet nuclear explosions. These high-altitude balloons allegedly contained not only scientific equipment, but purportedly contained anthropomorphic dummies. The dummies were somehow placed in the balloon capsule and were probably instrumented, although we do not really know. The balloon crashed in Roswell (somewhat near the Alamogordo, airbase) and as a result, there was a big pile of equipment from the capsule and the remains of the supposed anthropomorphic dummies. So rumors started spreading that the capsule itself with all the ancillary equipment was actually a UFO, and the anthropomorphic dummies were aliens from outer space. Who knows where the real truth lies? But all the alien rumors are fantastic tourist attractions for the city of Roswell.

ChatGPT output:

The Truth Behind Roswell's Extraterrestrial Misadventure: A Cosmic Comedy

In the vast and mysterious universe, there exists a little town called Roswell, New Mexico, where the tales of green beings with massive eyes and questionable fashion sense have woven themselves into the fabric of local lore. But let's delve beyond the conspiracy theories and into the realm of reality, or as close to it as we can get when discussing alien invasions.

Picture it: 1947. The world was still reeling from the aftermath of World War II, and humanity was collectively holding its breath, waiting for the next big thing to come crashing down. Little did they know that thing would be a high-altitude balloon, not a spaceship.

Enter the United States Army Air Corps, with their ingenious plan to spy on the Soviets by floating anthropomorphic dummies high above the Earth's surface. Why anthropomorphic dummies, you ask? Well, why not? It's not like they could send Brad Pitt or Scarlett Johansson up there to wave at the Russians. So, dummies it was.

These brave, plastic pioneers were loaded onto high-altitude balloons along with some fancy scientific equipment, and off they went, soaring into the heavens like the world's least intimidating superhero team. But alas, fate had other plans.

Somewhere over the deserts of Roswell, New Mexico, disaster struck. Whether it was a sudden gust of wind or an ill-timed bird strike, we may never know, but the balloon came crashing down to Earth, scattering its cargo of dummies and gadgets across the landscape like a cosmic yard sale.

Now, picture yourself as a curious Roswellian, stumbling upon this scene of chaos and confusion. You see strange debris scattered about, and in the distance, a group of military personnel scurrying around, looking just as bewildered as you feel. What's a rational explanation for all this? Clearly, it's aliens.

And thus, the legend of the Roswell UFO was born. Rumors spread like wildfire, fueled by imagination and a healthy dose of paranoia. Suddenly, every odd-shaped rock and stray piece of tinfoil became evidence of extraterrestrial visitation, and Roswell found itself thrust into the spotlight of intergalactic intrigue.

But let's not dismiss the power of a good story, especially when it comes to tourism. Roswell may not have little green men roaming its streets (at least, not that we know of), but it does have a thriving industry built on the back of its otherworldly reputation. Alien-themed cafes, souvenir shops stocked with all manner of space-themed trinkets, and an annual UFO festival that's out of this world (pun intended) – Roswell has turned a potential PR disaster into a cosmic cash cow.

So, what's the truth behind Roswell's alleged close encounter of the third kind? Was it a top-secret government experiment gone awry, or did little green men really crash-land in the desert? The answer, my friends, is blowing in the wind, along with the remnants of that ill-fated balloon.

As for the real aliens, well, who's to say they're not still out there, lurking in the shadows of Area 51, sipping alien cocktails and laughing at our feeble attempts to uncover the truth? Until they decide to reveal themselves (or until we stumble upon another crashed balloon), we'll just have to keep looking to the stars and wondering what else might be lurking in the vast expanse of the cosmos.

My comments:

This chat output was surprisingly good. It seemed to reject or overlook the purpose of the balloon of detecting Russian nuclear testing. It also implied the balloon was possibly traveling over Russia, when in reality it was in the desert of the American southwest. I enjoyed the addition of Brad Pitt and Scarlett Johansson and admired the phrase "like a cosmic yard sale". This story reinforces a trend that when chat seems to know a lot about a subject it does a better job.

MY INPUT: The family vacation at their favorite condo

Please write a humorous and comic story about . . . A resort vacation with the family.

Tell about the check in line at registration and getting a unit that has a prime view of the dumpsters. Go back to the front desk to get another unit. Meanwhile, the kids are yelling yes, they want to go to the pool.

The seven-year-old opened the bedroom door and ran 75 mph all the way from the living room through the dining room and flew through the air onto the bed—and then repeated this 17 times. The next guests may be wondering why there's a big dip in the mattress.

The boys and the girls fought with stuffed toys in the living room and, of course, one gets hit too hard and goes crying to mom.

The dishwasher was loaded with dirty dishes desperately needed for the next day and it didn't work. Of course, it only happened at 11:30 pm. Breakfast with dirty dishes?

The young boy chased older sister, with a booger on the end of his finger. The girl screamed, and the boy had this huge smile on his face.

The young boy shot a Nerf gun and bounced Nerf bullets off the living room ceiling. Later, he shot the Nerf bullets off the ceiling of his parents' bedroom and his dad found, quite surprisingly, that he had been sleeping with a Nerf bullet for the whole night.

And they call this a vacation???

ChatGPT output:

The Johnson family had been eagerly anticipating their resort vacation for months. They had visions of lazy days by the pool, indulging in delicious food, and making precious memories together. However, reality had other plans in store for them.

As they arrived at the resort, the check-in line seemed longer than the Great Wall of China, and the kids were already bouncing off the walls with excitement. Finally reaching the front desk, they were handed the keys to their unit, only to discover upon arrival that their "scenic view" was of the resort's dumpsters. Back to the front desk they went, hoping for better luck the second time around.

With a new room secured, they unpacked their belongings, but before they could even catch their breath, chaos ensued. Their seven-year-old, fueled by a mixture of adrenaline and sugar, transformed into a human tornado, streaking through the living room at lightning speed and crash-landing onto the bed like a superhero in training. The poor mattress would never be the same again.

Meanwhile, the boys and girls engaged in a fierce battle of stuffed toys, which inevitably led to tears and accusations of unfair play. Amidst the chaos, the dishwasher decided to stage a rebellion, leaving the family with a sink full of dirty dishes and a sinking feeling that breakfast might be a bit more crunchy than they had hoped.

Adding to the madness, one of the younger boys, armed with a freshly excavated booger, decided to chase his older sister around the room, much to her horror and his delight. And just when they thought things couldn't get any wilder, another young adventurer discovered the joy of bouncing Nerf bullets off the ceiling, much to the dismay of his parents who found themselves dodging projectiles even in the sanctity of their own bedroom.

Despite the mayhem and madness, amidst the laughter and chaos, the Johnsons realized that this, indeed, was their vacation. Maybe not the serene retreat they had imagined, but a wild and unforgettable adventure, nonetheless. And as they collapsed onto their slightly lopsided mattress at the end of the day, they couldn't help but laugh at the absurdity of it all.

And so, they embraced the messiness of family vacations, knowing that sometimes the best memories are made in the most unexpected moments. And who needs a scenic view when you have a front-row seat to the greatest show on earth - the Johnson family vacation.

My comments:

This story was based on my personal experience! I have not edited it at all but if I were to edit it, I would add in the 75 miles an hour and jumping on the bed 17 times that chat deleted. Specific numbers are more humorous than general expressions. I should have added specific names to the boy and girl as it would have made this story better. It took roughly 2 seconds for chat to create the output.

MY INPUT: A humorous and comical story about humans and computers

Write a humorous and comical story about humans and computers. Use the exact title "human and computers – – the slightest mistake can be devastating." Computers can be a great help for mankind, but it's often easy to make a mistake by typing the wrong character or clicking on the wrong spot. I'm sure almost everybody has experienced some type of embarrassing mistake, but the following mistakes fall into a special category. My complete 2023 income tax forms including the basic 1040 and all the associated forms such as the itemized deductions and the like were completed using SpeedieTax software and somehow, they were erroneously sent to the 85 people on our Christmas card list! How embarrassing that 85 people now know my finances such as salary, investments, investment losses and minor gains, and worst of all, my questionable deductions like how much I contributed or did not contribute to charity. They can tell a lot about my values by looking at my donations. Basically, my whole financial life was laid out in clear, straightforward terms. One of the worst experiences was when my wife placed an online order for some pink lacy "undies" where the shipping address was inadvertently selected to be that of my boss! How do you recover from this type of mistake? Do you pray for a loss package? Do you hope for a porch pirate incident? Or do you actually hire a porch pirate to do the dirty work?

The last mistake was the most emotional mistake. It almost came to a physical fight. My wife was working toward her masters in family and marriage counseling and had just finished 25 pages of the final report for her final class. Of course, she did not back it up because I did not explain to her how to back up documents. You may be guessing the next step. Inadvertently, the whole 25 pages of non-backed-up data got erroneously deleted. This represented three weeks of significant work and many hours, much of it written from 4 AM to 6 AM in the morning when the house was quiet. I don't recall how this incident ended. It could've been one of my emergency visits to the local hospital or it could've ended in five sessions of marriage counseling. I don't remember probably because my brain had been turned to Jell-O over this incident.

ChatGPT Output

Human and Computers – The Slightest Mistake Can Be Devastating

In the grand theater of life, humans and computers often share the stage, dancing a tango of errors and mishaps that can leave one laughing or crying—or both. Take, for instance, the tale of Bob, a hapless individual whose misadventures in the realm of technology led to a series of comical catastrophes.

It all began innocently enough, as many calamities do. Bob, armed with nothing but good intentions and a penchant for procrastination, decided to tackle his income tax forms using the trusty SpeedieTax software. Little did he know that with one misplaced click, his financial secrets would be broadcast to the world—or at least to the 85 people on his Christmas card list. Suddenly, Bob found himself in the unenviable position of having his entire financial life laid bare before his friends, family, and acquaintances, like a squirrel caught raiding the nut stash.

But Bob's troubles were just beginning. In a stroke of cosmic irony, his wife, in a moment of online shopping frenzy, managed to send a package of lacy pink undies to none other than Bob's boss. As visions of awkward office encounters danced in his head, Bob pondered his options: pray for a lost package, hope for a porch pirate intervention, or perhaps even consider hiring a nefarious thief to abscond with the embarrassing undergarments—a plan so ludicrous it just might work.

Yet, it was the final fiasco that truly tested Bob's resolve and his marriage. As his wife neared the completion of her master's degree in family and marriage counseling, disaster struck in the form of a deleted 25-page final report. Hours of meticulous work vanished into the digital ether, leaving Bob and his wife in a state of panic and despair. Amidst the chaos, Bob couldn't recall whether the ordeal ended with a trip to the hospital or a series of counseling sessions, his brain reduced to a quivering mass of gelatinous uncertainty.

Through it all, Bob learned a valuable lesson: in the delicate dance between humans and computers, the slightest misstep can have consequences both hilarious and heartbreaking. But with perseverance, a healthy dose of humor, and perhaps a few extra backups, even the most devastating mistakes can be overcome—or at the very least, turned into fodder for dinner party anecdotes. After all, what's life without a little laughter and a lot of lacy underwear mishaps?

My Comments:

This output needs to have many of the original details added back in such as 85 folks knowing his salary, investment losses, deductions and the 4:00 am to 6:00 am fiasco. The chat writing flows easily, but key, specific humorous items did not get picked up. However chat did include the complexity and the frustrations of humans and computers attempting to work together.

MY INPUT: Conference call background noises

In the modern world of working from home and global connectivity, we are frequently on audio conference calls. There are many background noises, both common and unusual, that can be heard during these conversations. They include sounds from vacuum cleaners, doing dishes, a pet parrot screeching in the background, and even a rooster crowing when one person is working remotely from the Philippines. The various sounds even include that of a baby because the baby is being held on the mother's lap, of dogs barking, of cats purring, and the occasional siren from an ambulance or a firetruck (everybody wants to stop the business conversation and ask what's happening with the firetruck or the ambulance). Please write a humorous comical piece about these fascinating sounds.

ChatGPT Output:

Ah, the symphony of modern work-from-home life! It's like a cacophony of chaos and comedy, all rolled into one conference call. Picture this: you're trying to discuss quarterly reports with your team, but instead of the soothing sounds of productivity, you're serenaded by a parade of peculiar noises.

First up, we have the vacuum cleaner, the unsung hero of domestic multitasking. It's like a background beat, reminding us that while we're discussing marketing strategies, someone's also tackling the dust bunnies.

Then there's the clatter of dishes being washed, a rhythmic reminder that even during business hours, the kitchen is still open for business. It's like a culinary percussion section, providing a steady rhythm for your meeting.

And let's not forget about our feathered friends. The parrot squawking in the background adds a tropical flair to the proceedings. It's like having a wild jungle adventure while discussing budget forecasts.

Now, imagine you're in a call with your colleague from the Philippines, and suddenly, a rooster crows in the background. It's like a wake-up call for everyone involved, reminding us that no matter where we are, nature always has a voice in the conversation.

Of course, we can't overlook the baby babbling away in the background. It's like a cute little interruption, reminding us that even in the midst of business, there's always room for a bit of family time.

And then there are the pets. Dogs barking, cats purring—it's like a virtual pet parade, with each furry friend vying for attention in the spotlight.

But perhaps the most unexpected guest of all is the distant wail of an ambulance or firetruck. Suddenly, the business conversation grinds to a halt as everyone scrambles to find out what's happening outside someone's window. It's like a suspenseful plot twist in the midst of an otherwise mundane meeting.

So, the next time you find yourself on a conference call surrounded by a symphony of strange sounds, just embrace the chaos and remember in the world of remote work, every noise has its own comedic charm

My comments:

This is one of the best chat outputs ever! Well written with chat even generating words on its own such as "budget forecasts" and "marketing strategies". Part of the reason for the quality output may have been the more specific input. The real moral of this story—don't worry about odd background noises as all conference calls have some!

ChatGPT Output:

Tails of Tails: An Epic Anthology of Animal Antics

In a quaint suburban neighborhood where lawns are neatly manicured and mailboxes stand in orderly rows, there exists a world of chaos and comedy known only to the furry inhabitants and their long-suffering human companions. Welcome, dear readers, to a collection of pet peeves and purr-fectly hilarious pet stories, where the antics of our four-legged friends reign supreme.

Our journey begins with the tale of Mr. Whiskers, a mischievous tabby with a penchant for mischief and mayhem. No vase is safe from his curious paws, no curtain unclimbable for his adventurous spirit. But despite his penchant for causing chaos, Mr. Whiskers is beloved by his human, Mrs. Jenkins, who finds herself constantly swept up in his whirlwind of furry antics.

Next, we encounter the saga of Barkley, a lovable but clueless golden retriever whose enthusiasm knows no bounds. From mistaking the mail carrier for a rival squirrel to accidentally ingesting an entire bag of flour and leaving a trail of paw prints throughout the house, Barkley's escapades never fail to elicit laughter (and exasperation) from his long-suffering owners.

But perhaps the most uproarious tale of all is that of Sir Reginald, a pompous and persnickety Persian cat with a taste for the finer things in life. From turning up his nose at anything less than gourmet cat food to demanding his own velvet-lined throne for napping, Sir Reginald's diva-like behavior knows no bounds. Yet, despite his airs and graces, he never fails to provide his human, Lord Montague, with endless amusement (and the occasional headache).

As we delve deeper into the world of animal antics, we encounter a colorful cast of characters, from the mischievous ferrets who turn their owner's sock drawer into a chaotic playground to the eccentric parrot who insists on reciting Shakespearean soliloquies at all hours of the day and night.

But amidst the chaos and comedy, there is a profound bond that unites these disparate creatures with their human companions. For in the end, it is the unconditional love and companionship of our furry friends that make even the most exasperating pet peeves worth enduring.

So here's to the pets who turn our lives upside down with their antics, who fill our days with laughter and our hearts with joy. May their tails wag and their purrs rumble on, bringing light and laughter to our lives for years to come.

My comments:

Chat's humor sparkled with the sentence, "... eccentric parrot who insists on reciting Shakespearean soliloquies at all hours of the day and night". Overall, I expected more from chat as pets are a rich source of humor. A missed opportunity? I should have guided chat with a more detailed input. Minor comment: Sir Reginald is male, yet chat used the term "diva-like" which implies female.

MY INPUT: The devious people who design medical equipment (especially MRIs)

Write about the devious people who design medical equipment and medical procedures. For example, the people that invented and perfected MRI machines studied which noises and combination of noises, intensity of noises and frequency of noises that most bothered the human brain, and then they designed that irritating set of noises into the MRI machine.

Another example is the people who designed equipment to detect cancer in women's breasts. They originally had a device that was comfortable, but then the devious ideas came to mind where they made an uncomfortable x-ray process which, of course, they claimed was more accurate than the comfortable process. Hence the modern mammogram!

Now enter the whole area of nuclear imaging. First, let's call it "nuclear" imaging so they can scare people with some kind of wild danger from a nuclear device. At a minimum, scare people into thinking they may glow in the dark. Then give them an injection that takes an hour to circulate throughout their body. Take the nuclear injection material out of a special lead box that will scare them into thinking it's super radioactive.

Now write a humors article about these inventive and devious people who design these types of medical equipment and procedures.

ChatGPT output:

The Mad Scientists of Medicine: Unraveling the Devious Designs Behind Medical Equipment

In the shadowy corridors of medical innovation, where white lab coats mingle with flashes of inspiration and a touch of madness, there exists a breed of inventor unlike any other. Meet the devious geniuses behind the design of medical equipment and procedures, whose twisted minds concoct the most diabolical devices known to modern medicine.

Our journey into the depths of medical mischief begins with the MRI machine, a marvel of modern technology and a torture chamber for the senses. Little did we know that behind its sleek exterior lies a symphony of cacophonous chaos carefully crafted to torment the human brain. Yes, dear readers, those devious designers actually studied which noises, frequencies, and intensities would most perturb our delicate psyche, and then gleefully incorporated them into the MRI's repertoire of auditory torment. It's as if they took a page straight out of a supervillain's playbook, transforming a routine medical procedure into a psychological thriller worthy of Hitchcock himself.

But wait, it gets even more sinister. Consider the case of the mammogram, a seemingly innocuous procedure designed to detect breast cancer. At first glance, one might assume that comfort and compassion would guide the design process. Oh, how wrong we would be. Instead, the nefarious minds behind the modern mammogram took a perfectly pleasant process and twisted it into a discomforting ordeal of squishing and squeezing, all in the name of supposed accuracy. It's as if they relish in the suffering of their unsuspecting subjects, turning a routine screening into a harrowing journey through the valley of discomfort.

And let's not forget about nuclear imaging, a realm where fear and fascination collide in a radioactive dance of dread. From its ominous moniker to the foreboding lead-lined boxes that house its radioactive injections, every aspect of nuclear imaging seems designed to strike fear into the hearts of its hapless participants. It's as if the designers took inspiration from a Cold War-era horror film, conjuring visions of glowing green goo and mutant creatures lurking in the shadows.

But amidst the madness and mayhem, there is a twisted brilliance to be found in the minds of these medical mavericks. For it is their devious designs that push the boundaries of what is possible, driving innovation forward in the quest for better health and healing. So here's to the mad scientists of medicine, the architects of agony and the purveyors of pain, whose diabolical creations remind us that sometimes, the path to progress is paved with a touch of madness.

My comments:

Chat followed my input well; however I think the "green goo" analogy went a bit too far. It sometimes takes significant guidance to have chat write what you want with humor. In the input, I should have added and highlighted the "tiny diameter" of the MRI tube that occasionally sends patients into claustrophobia fits. It would have been fun to see what chat would have done with this confined space challenge.

MY INPUT: The day before the Super Bowl at Safemarket

On the day before the Super Bowl, Safemarket is a hazardous place. Customers are frantic trying to get everything they need. There were five carts that crashed in the beer aisle because the men have been grabbing six packs, not looking where they're going. On the way to the chip aisle, two carts were racing when they turned the corner on two wheels and saw two carts flipped over and entangled right by the Late July jalapeño chips.

In the refrigerated dip aisle, the yummy dips were out of stock. Frantic Super Bowl fans were struggling to find alternatives since cream cheese or possibly whipped cottage cheese could be doctored up with dried jalapeños. Cruising by the fruit and vegetables, no carts could be observed. Not a single person was in the vegetable or fruit department— not even in front of the mixed vegetables with the dip in the center. OK, On the way to the wine department, several carts had crashed in front of the hard liquor area. The crashed seemed to be concentrated in the tequila row. Because of the massive crowds, many Super Bowl fans had decided to use the self-service checkout. In the midst of the self-service checkout, a grumpy supermarket clerk stopped by and said it's against the law to self-check-out alcohol, so this huge disappointment forced the football fans to go to the back of a massive line that extended halfway down the cereal aisle. After 45 minutes of waiting in line, finally, the Super Bowl rush was over.

Write an extremely humorous article about the above Super Bowl experience in the supermarket.

ChatGPT Output

"Super Bowl Chaos: Supermarket Shenanigans Reach Epic Proportions"

In what can only be described as a clash of titans, the day before the Super Bowl transformed Safemarket into a battlefield of beer, chips, and chaos.

As unsuspecting shoppers innocently navigated the aisles in search of game day essentials, they found themselves thrust into a comedic saga worthy of its own halftime show.

Picture this: five carts collide in a spectacular showdown worthy of a demolition derby, all because grown men were too fixated on snagging six-packs to bother with basic cart-driving etiquette. Meanwhile, two carts engage in a high-speed race to the chip aisle, executing a flawless turn only to witness a crash of epic proportions in front of the Late July corn and chia chips.

But the drama doesn't stop there. In the refrigerated dip aisle, panic ensues as fans discover the unthinkable – the coveted yummy dips are nowhere to be found. With cream cheese and whipped cottage cheese as their only hope, shoppers contemplate desperate dip alternatives, including a daring attempt to doctor up their dairy delights with dried jalapeños.

As if that wasn't enough, the fruit and vegetable department resembles a ghost town, with not a single soul in sight – not even in front of the mixed vegetables with dip in the center, a rare gem left untouched amidst the madness. Meanwhile, the wine department witnesses a different kind of wreckage, as carts collide in a chaotic dance, with tequila-fueled crashes stealing the spotlight.

But the pièce de résistance comes at the self-service checkout, where a grumpy supermarket clerk delivers a crushing blow to the hopes of eager fans. With a stern declaration that self-checking out alcohol is against the law, the football faithful are forced to abandon ship and join a line that rivals the length of a football field, stretching halfway down the cereal aisle.

After 45 minutes of waiting, with the tension palpable enough to rival any fourth-quarter nail-biter, the Super Bowl rush finally comes to an end. As shoppers emerge victorious, clutching their chips, beer, and hastily acquired dip substitutes, they can't help but laugh at the absurdity of it all.

And thus, another Super Bowl shopping saga goes down in supermarket history, leaving us all with a tale to tell and a newfound appreciation for the chaos of game day prep.

My comments:

This output was excellent and realistically described the craziness of Super Bowl shoppers. Chat seemed confused as the input described the tequila row but instead of a location chat jumped to "with tequila-fueled crashes stealing the spotlight." A hallucination? Chat was probably statistically trained more on people drinking tequila rather than tequila helping describe a supermarket location. Or maybe chat was drinking too much tequila!

MY INPUT: The wonders and pitfalls of online dating

Write an extremely humorous article about the wonders and pitfalls of online dating. Use lots of examples.

ChatGPT output:

The Rollercoaster of Online Dating: A Hilarious Ride Through the Wonders and Pitfalls

Welcome, brave souls, to the wild and wacky world of online dating! Buckle up, because we're about to embark on a rollercoaster ride filled with laughter, tears, and a whole lot of swiping left and right.

Let's start with the wonders, shall we? Picture this: you're lounging on your couch in your pajamas, armed with nothing but your trusty smartphone and a steaming cup of coffee. With a few taps of your finger, you're suddenly thrust into a virtual smorgasbord of potential romantic partners, each one more intriguing than the last. It's like shopping for love in the convenience aisle of the internet, and boy, is it exhilarating!

But hold onto your hats, folks, because where there are wonders, there are also pitfalls aplenty. Take, for instance, the dreaded ghosting phenomenon. One minute, you're engaged in a riveting conversation with a charming stranger, exchanging witty banter and emojis galore. The next? Radio silence. Your messages float into the digital abyss, never to be seen or heard from again. It's like being stood up at the altar, only without the benefit of a free meal.

And let's not forget about the perils of misrepresentation. You know the drill: you come across a profile picture that could rival the Mona Lisa in its beauty, only to discover upon meeting in person that your date resembles more of a Picasso painting. Cue the awkward small talk and desperate attempts to find an escape route, pronto.

But fear not, dear readers, for amidst the chaos and confusion of online dating, there are moments of sheer hilarity that make it all worthwhile. Like the time you accidentally matched with your ex's best friend's cousin's roommate and spent the entire evening swapping horror stories about your mutual connection. Or when you stumbled upon a profile that boasted a love for long walks on the beach and synchronized swimming with dolphins (hey, to each their own!).

And let's not overlook the joy of discovering a fellow aficionado of obscure '90s sitcoms or a kindred spirit who shares your affinity for cheesy pickup lines. Who knew that "Are you a magician? Because whenever I look at you, everyone else disappears" could be the catalyst for a lifelong romance?

So there you have it, folks: the wonders and pitfalls of online dating, wrapped up in a neat little package of laughter and absurdity. So next time you find yourself navigating the murky waters of the digital dating scene, remember to approach it with equal parts optimism and a healthy dose of humor. After all, as they say, "Love may be just a click away, but a good laugh is priceless."

My comments:

Not bad at all but chat could have "created" many more examples and stories of super matches, rapid break ups, and more regular matches. A genuine missed opportunity! Chat did come up with a fascinating comparison using the Mona Lisa vs. a Picasso to describe a person's appearance.

MY INPUT: Renting a car at the airport

Write a humorous and comical article about the frustrations of renting a car at the airport. Start with the on-line reservation process to select your class of car such as a RAV-4 or a luxury Lincoln Town car or a large Suburban SUV. They show the price but hold on—that's only the rice of the car and not the "secret" add on's that are only reviled later. For example, a $500 car fee after the concession recovery fee and the vehicle license recoup fee and the state tourist fee as well as local airport taxes and state taxes are added winds up to be a whopping $779.

The next challenge is finding the car amidst the massive, dark three-story lot. It should be so simple —just go to space B 216 but B216 is 3/4 of a mile at the end of the lot hidden behind a massive pillar. And this, of course, is when you're in a hurry.

Once you find the car you have to figure out how it works. Cars are no longer have consistent human oriented ergonomic design. Your rental car is guaranteed not to work like your personal car. First you have to find the mirror adjustment lever. It seems to be always hidden in the darkest part of the armrest and then, is it a lever or is it a knob that turns? And the greatest challenge is finding the gear shift mechanism and getting used to how it works. In some cars it is a set of push buttons where you push one button for drive, but you have to **pull** other buttons such as for reverse. Whoever decided push buttons were great way to shift gears? And then other cars have a rotating dial. Rotate it all the way clockwise for drive— other positions for other gears. All these combinations are conceptually not bad, but they are the antithesis of what your muscle memory tells you about how to shift the car. Finally, there's the parking brake. Some cars now have a push button, and others have a simulated brake handle where you pull the handle which is just a push button in disguise. Some have the brake on the far-left lower part of the dashboard and some have it on the console between the seats. Are the human factor designers of cars evil people or do they just think about what looks good with no regard to what human beings need or are used to.

ChatGPT output:

Navigating the Hilarious Maze of Airport Car Rentals

So, you've booked your rental car online, dreaming of cruising in a sleek RAV-4 or luxuriating in a Lincoln Town Car. The price looks reasonable, you think you've got this in the bag. But hold your horses, my friend, because the real adventure is just beginning.

As you approach the rental counter, you start to feel a twinge of apprehension. The agent greets you with a smile, but behind that smile lurks the ominous specter of hidden fees. Suddenly, your $500 rental morphs into a monstrous $779 beast, courtesy of concession recovery fees, vehicle license recovery fees, state tourist fees, local airport taxes, and a partridge in a pear tree.

Undeterred by the financial slap to your wallet, you embark on the next leg of your journey: finding your chariot amidst the labyrinthine parking lot. Space B216 beckons like a siren in the distance, but as you trudge through the vast expanse of asphalt, reality sinks in. B216 might as well be in Narnia, hidden behind pillars and tucked away in the shadows, mocking your sense of direction and urgency.

But wait, you've finally stumbled upon your chosen steed, only to realize that deciphering its inner workings is akin to cracking the Da Vinci code. Mirror adjustment levers lurk in the darkest recesses of armrests, mocking your attempts at ergonomic logic. Is it a lever? Is it a knob? Who knows, it's a mystery wrapped in an enigma.

And let's not even start on the gear shift mechanism. Push buttons, rotating dials, simulated brake handles—oh my! Whoever thought push buttons were a brilliant idea for shifting gears clearly never had to navigate rush hour traffic in a foreign city. Your muscle memory rebels against these alien contraptions, leaving you feeling like a novice driver all over again.

And what's the deal with parking brakes? Push buttons, simulated handles, dashboard appendages—each rental car seems determined to outdo the other in terms of sheer absurdity. Are the designers evil geniuses, or do they simply revel in our collective confusion?

As you finally navigate out of the parking lot, you can't help but chuckle at the absurdity of it all. Sure, renting a car at the airport may be a comedy of errors, but hey, at least it makes for a good story. And who knows, maybe one day you'll look back on this experience and laugh, preferably from the comfort of your own, familiar car.

My comments:

The smooth flow of chat's writings surprised to me and impressed me. However, it did not include many details I thought were important. I wrote the lengthy input because there are so many required steps to renting a car. The phrase "simulated brake handles" does not belong in the gear shift sentence. This is out of context. However, I commend chat for the phrase, "... clearly never had to navigate rush hour traffic in a foreign city". This foreign city phrase definitely indicates chat understands the context and the muscle memory element of stressful driving in new situations.

MY INPUT: Rewrite this rental car article as if it were written by a sixth-grade student

ChatGPT output:

The Wacky Adventure of Renting a Car

So, like, you're all excited 'cause you booked this cool car online, right? You're thinking, "Yeah, I'm gonna drive in style!" But then, when you get to the airport to pick it up, it's like a whole big crazy thing!

First, you go to the counter, and the person there is smiling, but then they start adding all these extra fees. Suddenly, your $500 car turns into a monster that eats up $779! What a bummer, right?

Then, you have to find your car in this ginormous parking lot. They tell you it's in space B216, but getting there feels like you're on a treasure hunt in a maze. And of course, you're in a hurry, so it's even more stressful!

Finally, you find your car, but now you gotta figure out how it works. The mirrors are like, hidden in the darkest corners, and the gear shift thingy is all weird. Some cars have buttons for shifting gears, others have this spinning thing, and it's so confusing!

And don't even get me started on the parking brake! It's like they're playing a prank on us. Some cars have a button, some have a fake handle, and others put it in the weirdest spots.

Seriously, who comes up with this stuff? It's like they're trying to make it as tricky as possible just to mess with us! But hey, at least it makes for a funny story to tell later, right? Gotta laugh at the craziness of it all!

My comments:

Rewriting stories as if they were written by either a six-grade student or a college professor is a genuine strength of chat and a powerful function. I love the words, "thingy" and "ginormous"! Obviously, chat has been hanging out with a lot of 6th grade students.

ChatGPT output

(an original case with no input shown)

Unraveling the Mysteries of Egyptian Pyramid Construction: A Humorous Exploration

Ah, the pyramids of Egypt! Majestic, awe-inspiring... and utterly confounding. How on earth did ancient Egyptians manage to stack massive stone blocks on top of each other with such precision? Let's dive into the hilarious world of pyramid construction and uncover the truth behind the monumental mystery.

Picture this: a bunch of ancient Egyptians sitting around, scratching their heads, and pondering the age-old question, "How do we build a pyramid?" Naturally, someone suggests, "Let's just stack a bunch of rocks on top of each other and see what happens!" And thus, the construction of the pyramids was born... probably.

Now, let's address the elephant in the room: aliens. Yep, you heard me right. Some people genuinely believe that aliens swooped down from outer space and lent a hand (or several tentacles) in building these massive structures. I mean, it's as good an explanation as any, right? After all, who wouldn't want to imagine ancient Egyptians having interstellar construction buddies?

But let's get real for a moment. The truth is probably a lot less extraterrestrial and a lot more... human. Maybe they had a pyramid-building competition, complete with teams of ancient Egyptian engineers, architects, and laborers, all vying for the title of "Pharaoh's Favorite Builder." Think Olympics, but with more sand and fewer gold medals.

Of course, no humorous exploration of pyramid construction would be complete without a nod to the ol' "slave labor" theory. Sure, it's a bit dark, but hey, we're talking about ancient history here, folks. Let's just hope they at least provided the slaves with some decent pyramid-building music to keep their spirits up. Can you imagine a bunch of workers belting out "Walk Like an Egyptian" while hauling giant stone blocks? Talk about motivation!

And let's not forget the age-old question: how did they move those massive stones? Some say they used ramps, while others swear by the power of mind control (okay, maybe not, but you get the idea). Personally, I like to imagine them employing a fleet of specially trained camels with impeccable strength and balance. Hey, a girl can dream, right?

So there you have it, folks. The hilarious world of pyramid construction: where aliens, pyramid-building competitions, slave labor, and super-powered camels all come together in a delightful blend of historical absurdity. As for the real answer? Well, that's a mystery that's still waiting to be uncovered... preferably with a side of laughter.

My comments:

Remarkable job of discussing the various pyramid construction theories.

ChatGPT output:

The Funny Story of How Pyramids Were Built

Okay, so picture this: ancient Egypt, right? They're all like, "Let's build some big pointy things!" But like, how do you even do that? Well, let me tell you, it's a pretty funny story.

First off, some people think aliens helped out. Yeah, aliens! Like, little green guys with spaceships and stuff. Maybe they were bored and decided to build some cool stuff on Earth. Who knows, right? It's a wild idea, but hey, anything's possible!

But then there's the idea that they had a big competition. Like, teams of Egyptians racing to see who could stack the most rocks. Can you imagine? It's like the Olympics, but with stones instead of medals. I bet they had pyramid-building music playing to keep them pumped up. Maybe they even danced while they worked!

And get this: some people say slaves did all the work. That's kinda sad, but hey, it's history, right? Maybe they had secret dance parties at night to keep their spirits up. Who knows?

Oh, and let's not forget about moving those giant rocks. Some say they used ramps, others think they had super strong camels. Yeah, camels! Maybe they had special training and everything. I like to think they wore little construction hats too. Adorable, right?

So yeah, building pyramids was a pretty wacky adventure. Whether it was aliens, competitions, or dancing camels, one thing's for sure: those ancient Egyptians knew how to make history funny!

My comments:

Definitely written by a 6th grade student.

ChatGPT output:

Exploring the Enigmatic Origins of Pyramid Construction: An Academic Examination

In the annals of human history, few architectural marvels rival the grandeur and mystery of the Egyptian pyramids. Yet, the question of how these colossal structures were erected remains a subject of scholarly debate and speculation. In this discourse, we shall endeavor to dissect the various theories surrounding pyramid construction with a critical lens, while acknowledging the inherent complexity and uncertainty of the subject matter.

At the forefront of pyramid construction theories lies the notion of extraterrestrial intervention, positing that advanced beings from beyond our planet assisted in the erection of these monumental edifices. While this hypothesis captivates the imagination and has garnered widespread popular appeal, it lacks empirical evidence and fails to withstand rigorous scientific scrutiny.

Alternatively, proponents of the internal workforce model assert that a vast labor force, comprised predominantly of enslaved individuals, was mobilized to undertake the arduous task of pyramid construction under the direction of skilled overseers. While historical records and archaeological evidence lend credence to the existence of a labor force, the extent of coercion and the logistical feasibility of such an endeavor remain subjects of contention.

Another prevalent theory suggests the implementation of innovative engineering techniques, such as the employment of ramps and pulleys, to transport and maneuver the massive stone blocks used in pyramid construction. While this theory offers a plausible explanation for the logistical challenges posed by the transportation of stone blocks, the precise methodologies employed and the practicalities of their execution remain elusive.

Additionally, the possibility of interdynastic competition driving pyramid construction efforts cannot be discounted. It is conceivable that rival pharaohs sought to assert their dominance and immortalize their legacies through the erection of increasingly grandiose monuments, thereby fueling a competitive race to build ever larger and more elaborate pyramids.

Ultimately, the true origins of pyramid construction likely encompass a multifaceted interplay of socio-political, cultural, and technological factors. While each theory offers valuable insights into the complexities of ancient Egyptian civilization, the enigma of pyramid construction persists as a testament to the ingenuity and resourcefulness of humanity throughout the ages.

My comments:

Chat skillfully nailed the academic style. Now let's retreat to the faculty club for a drink.

MY INPUT: **A story about the constitutional convention**

Write a humorous, comical story about the constitutional convention and all the battles about large state small states, freeman and slaves, and the environment of Philadelphia in the summer—the outrageous heat.

ChatGPT output:

A Hilarious Tale of the Constitutional Convention

Gather 'round, dear readers, for a rib-tickling journey back to the sweltering summer of 1787 in the City of Brotherly Love, where the Constitutional Convention unfolded amidst a cacophony of debates, disagreements, and downright absurdity.

Picture this: Philadelphia, a city simmering under the blazing sun, with delegates sweating buckets in their powdered wigs and stuffy suits. It was hotter than a pepper sprout, and tensions were running higher than Ben Franklin's kite during a lightning storm.

Now, imagine a bunch of delegates from big states and little states, all squabbling like siblings fighting over the last cookie. The big states were like, "We should get more representation!" And the little states were all, "No way, Jose! We want equal footing!" It was like a political showdown at the OK Corral, but with quills instead of pistols.

And let's not forget about the whole freemen versus slaves debacle. Some delegates were all for freedom and equality, while others were clinging to their slaves like they were going out of style. Talk about awkward dinner conversation!

But amidst the chaos and heat-induced delirium, there were moments of pure comedic gold. Like when Alexander Hamilton showed up to the convention wearing a coat made entirely of money. Seriously, the guy had more bling than a rapper at the Grammys. It was like he was trying to bribe his way into the history books!

And then there was Benjamin Franklin, the wisest (and oldest) delegate in the room. He'd shuffle in, looking like he'd just rolled out of bed, and drop some profound wisdom like it was no big deal. I swear, the guy had more quotable lines than a Shakespeare play.

But perhaps the most hilarious moment of all was when they finally hammered out the Constitution and decided to break for lunch. You could practically hear the collective sigh of relief as delegates stumbled out of the stifling convention hall, desperate for some fresh air and a cold drink. I bet they were all thinking, "Thank goodness that's over!"

So there you have it, folks: the Constitutional Convention, where the stakes were high, the tempers were higher, and the laughs were aplenty. It was a hot mess of politics, passion, and powdered wigs, but hey, at least they got the job done in the end. And for that, we salute them... and maybe crank up the air conditioning a notch or two.

My comments:

I'd say this was accurate yet with significant humor. Interesting how timely the large state versus the small state issue is.

MY INPUT: Creating the Panama Canal

Write a humorous comical article about all the complexities of creating a Panama Canal. Talk about the French and how French investors lost lots of money and how the lessons from the Suez Canal did not apply to Panama due to the jungle climate, the various illnesses, the snakes, and the mountains that had to be dug through. Talk about the US trying to decide between Panama and Nicaragua as the best place for the canal. Talk about Teddy Roosevelt's desire to rapidly proceed with the Panama location to quickly finish so that the United States could have access to a Navy that could cover both oceans. And be sure to cover all the difficulties like overcoming malaria and yellow fever and worker revolts. Also cover greedy Wall Street investors.

ChatGPT output:

A Hilarious Expedition Through the Panama Canal Saga

Ah, the Panama Canal, where dreams of maritime glory collided with the harsh realities of jungle warfare, snake-infested mountains, and Wall Street shenanigans. Strap in, folks, 'cause this is one wild ride through the canal's tumultuous history!

So, picture this: a bunch of French investors thinking they could conquer the world by building a canal through Panama. Spoiler alert: they couldn't. The jungle chewed them up and spit them out faster than you can say "sacre bleu!" It turns out, the lessons learned from the Suez Canal didn't quite apply to Panama's steamy, snake-filled terrain. Who knew?

Meanwhile, across the pond, the US was like, "Hey, we need a canal too!" But where to build it? Panama or Nicaragua? Decisions, decisions. Teddy Roosevelt, never one to shy away from a challenge, was all, "Let's go with Panama, folks! We need a shortcut to flex our naval muscles and dominate both oceans." Talk about ambitious!

But oh, the hurdles they faced. Malaria and yellow fever were more common than mosquitoes at a picnic, and worker revolts were as frequent as rainy days in the jungle. Greedy Wall Street investors were sniffing around like vultures, hoping to cash in on the canal's construction. It was like a real-life episode of "Survivor," but with Panama as the island and the contestants armed with shovels instead of immunity idols.

And let's not forget about the engineering marvels required to conquer Mother Nature's obstacles. Mountains had to be dug through, rivers rerouted, and locks built to lift ships up and over the rugged terrain. It was like a giant game of Jenga, but with ships instead of wooden blocks.

But you know what? They did it. Against all odds, the Panama Canal was completed, and the world was forever changed. Teddy Roosevelt got his shortcut, the US Navy got its access to both oceans, and Panama became synonymous with maritime ingenuity.

So here's to the Panama Canal, a testament to human perseverance, ingenuity, and the absurdity of trying to conquer nature with a bunch of shovels and a dream. Cheers to you, Panama!

My comments:

Chat did a good job with excellent phrasing. However, there were two exceptions. First, the "harsh realities of jungle warfare" was out of place as there was no warfare, and second, "Cheers to Panama" was a nice catchy phrase but it was France and the US that did the work and deserve the "cheers."

MY INPUT: The gunfight at OK corral

Write a humorous story about the gun fight at OK corral. Include the names of the participants and tell what they did years after the gunfight. Also, tell how many bullets were shot in a short period of time.

ChatGPT output:

In the dusty town of Tombstone, Arizona, the OK Corral was about to witness the most infamous 30 seconds in Wild West history. It was October 26, 1881, and tensions between the Earp brothers and the Clanton-McLaury gang had reached a boiling point.

Participants:

Wyatt Earp - The stoic lawman, who never smiled, even when he told a joke.

Virgil Earp - The elder brother, always trying to keep Wyatt out of trouble.

Morgan Earp - The youngest Earp, who believed in luck more than skill.

Doc Holliday - The gambler with a deadly cough and an even deadlier aim.

Ike Clanton - The loudmouth who never stopped talking, even during a gunfight.

Billy Clanton - Ike's younger brother, who was always cleaning up Ike's messes.

Tom McLaury - The quieter McLaury brother, always lurking in the background.

Frank McLaury - The more outspoken McLaury, who had a penchant for dramatic entrances.

As the clock struck high noon (or maybe it was a bit past, who really knows?), the Earps and Doc Holliday squared off against the Clantons and McLaurys in a narrow lot near the OK Corral. The tension was so thick, you could cut it with a butter knife. Suddenly, shots rang out. In just 30 seconds, more than 30 bullets were fired. It was a cacophony of chaos, with each participant shooting wildly, barely taking time to aim. Wyatt Earp, cool as a cucumber, fired his six-shooter with precision, managing to graze Ike Clanton's hat, sending it flying. Ike, startled, yelled, "You shot my favorite hat!" and took off running, never firing a single shot.

Virgil Earp took a bullet to the leg but continued to fire, hitting Tom McLaury in the shoulder. Tom, who was really just there for moral support, decided he'd had enough of this nonsense and crawled behind a horse trough. Morgan Earp, believing his luck was up, blindly fired over a barrel and, to his surprise, managed to hit Billy Clanton in the arm. Billy, ever the pragmatist, decided to sit down and contemplate his life choices while bleeding profusely. Doc Holliday, with a devilish grin, coughed his way through the fight, taking down Frank McLaury with a shot to the chest. Frank, ever the dramatic one, fell backward into a conveniently placed haystack, dramatically gasping, "Et tu, Doc?"

When the smoke cleared, the scene was a mix of the injured, the exhausted, and the exasperated. The townsfolk peered out from behind their shutters, wondering if it was safe to come out and sweep up the spent shells. Years later, the survivors of the gunfight led rather unexpected lives: Wyatt Earp moved to Hollywood, where he became a consultant for early Western films, often correcting directors with, "That's not how it happened, let me show you." Virgil Earp retired and opened a general store, where he was known for his grumpy yet fair prices. Morgan Earp took up poker, believing his luck had finally turned around. He became known as "Lucky Morgan," though he never quite understood why.

Doc Holliday continued gambling and coughing but also became a published author, writing a bestseller called "Coughing in the Wild West:

A Gambler's Guide." Ike Clanton moved to a quiet farm and never wore a hat again, fearing another close encounter with a bullet.

Billy Clanton became a peace advocate, traveling and giving lectures on the importance of not getting shot. Tom McLaury went into hiding, still traumatized by the horse trough incident. Frank McLaury's dramatic fall became a legendary tale, inspiring local theater productions for years.

And so, the gunfight at the OK Corral remained a legendary tale of wild shots, unexpected outcomes, and the quirky lives that followed.

My comments:

Wow! This was the best. I truly enjoyed reading all the encore careers, especially Wyatt Earp moving to Hollywood to become a consultant to early western films and Billy Clanton becoming a peace advocate giving lectures around the world. Another example of chat's exceptional writing ability.

MY INPUT: **The rapid construction of the Empire State Building**

Write a humorous, comical, and partly outrageous article about the construction of the Empire State Building. Discuss the fact that it needed no EPA Environmental Impact Reports and it had very few permits and the whole building was built in one year. Nowadays, it would take at least five years for the reports, the prerequisites and the paperwork before you even start construction. Discuss the ironworkers that walk on thin beams way up in the sky and don't fall down and are not afraid. Report on throwing red hot rivets yards away into a catching bucket. Be sure to include the emotion of the workers working up in the sky and the drama and excitement of the opening day.

ChatGPT output:

The Empire State Building: A Comedic Triumph of Steel and Guts

Step right up, folks, and prepare to be dazzled by the tale of the Empire State Building, a towering masterpiece born from steel, sweat, and sheer audacity. Strap in, 'cause this is one wild ride through the clouds!

First things first: back in the day, there were no pesky environmental impact reports or endless permits to worry about. Nope, they just rolled up their sleeves and got to work, like a bunch of over-caffeinated beavers building the world's tallest dam. Nowadays, you'd need a mountain of paperwork just to sneeze in the general direction of a construction site!

But let's talk about the real heroes of this story: the ironworkers. These guys had nerves of steel (pun intended) as they strolled along thin beams hundreds of feet in the air, defying gravity and common sense with every step. I mean, who needs a safety net when you've got a lunch pail and a devil-may-care attitude?

And let's not forget about those red-hot rivets flying through the air like fiery comets, only to be caught by fearless workers with hands of iron. Talk about a high-stakes game of catch! You couldn't pay me enough to play hot potato with molten metal, but these guys did it like it was just another day at the office.

Now, picture the scene on opening day: the city skyline ablaze with excitement as the Empire State Building loomed like a giant among skyscrapers. The crowds gathered, the champagne flowed, and the atmosphere crackled with electricity. It was like New Year's Eve, the Fourth of July, and Christmas morning all rolled into one.

And as the ribbon was cut and the doors swung open, the Empire State Building stood as a testament to human ingenuity, determination, and a healthy dose of insanity. Sure, it may have taken just one year to build, but the memories forged in those steel beams will last a lifetime.

So here's to the Empire State Building, a beacon of hope, a symbol of progress, and a damn fine piece of real estate. May it stand tall for centuries to come, a monument to the power of human ambition and the occasional disregard for safety regulations. Cheers to that!

My comments:

This writing was absolutely remarkable! It grasped the excitement of the construction and the opening. Enjoyable reading. One item where chat went astray was the bit about tossing red hot rivets. "Caught by fearless workers with *hands* of iron" is a hallucination as they were caught by metal buckets and not by hands. Also, the rivets were not "molten", which is a liquid state! Obviously, chat's training didn't include construction with rivets. Throwing hot "molten" liquid rivets 20 feet across a construction site sounds more like something out of a sci-fi novel.

MY INPUT: Humor and Antiques Roadshow

Write a humorous article about Antiques Roadshow, talk about silver antiques, gold antiques, Civil War guns and swords, Queen Anne furniture, jade pieces from China, New England Americana, and the like.

ChatGPT output:

The Shiny World of Antiques Roadshow: Where Silver Sparkles and Swords Speak

Ah, Antiques Roadshow, the treasure trove of eccentric items and the quintessential Sunday afternoon entertainment for those with a penchant for the past and a love for the quirky. Step into the world where silver isn't just for spoons, gold isn't just for jewelry, and even a humble chair can hold the secrets of centuries gone by.

Let's start with silver, shall we? It's not just about determining if your grandmother's tea set is worth a pretty penny; it's about the thrill of discovering that your tarnished trinket is actually a Tiffany masterpiece or that your dusty candlestick once graced the table of a queen (or at least a very fancy dinner party).

And then there's gold, the ultimate status symbol. But forget about flashy necklaces and gaudy rings; on Antiques Roadshow, gold takes on a whole new meaning. Think Civil War belt buckles, ancient coins, and intricately crafted artifacts that make Midas himself green with envy.

But it's not all about precious metals; the show dives into the depths of history with relics from the battlefield. Guns and swords from the Civil War era are prized possessions, each with its own story to tell. Who knew that your great-great-grandfather's rusty musket could hold such historical significance (and possibly value)?

Of course, no trip down the rabbit hole of antiques would be complete without a nod to the queen of the household: furniture. From Queen Anne chairs to ornate Victorian dressers, every piece has its own tale of craftsmanship and intrigue. And let's not forget the thrill of finding out that the rickety old chair gathering dust in your attic is actually a rare find worth enough to furnish a palace.

But the wonders of Antiques Roadshow aren't confined to the Western world. Jade pieces from China, with their delicate carvings and rich symbolism, transport viewers to the Far East with just a glance. Suddenly, that quirky figurine you picked up at a garage sale takes on a whole new level of significance.

And then there's New England, the heartland of Americana. From colonial-era relics to folk art masterpieces, each item is a testament to the rich tapestry of American history. Who knew that a simple quilt could hold the stories of generations past or that a weathered sign could be a window into a bygone era?

But amidst all the silver, gold, and historical artifacts, there's one thing that truly shines on Antiques Roadshow: the light. Not just any light, mind you, but the warm glow of nostalgia and the excitement of uncovering hidden treasures. So the next time you tune in to the show, remember it's not just about the antiques, it's about the journey. And maybe, just maybe, that dusty old relic in your attic could be the next star of the show.

My Comments:

Civil War belt buckles were not made of gold—looks like a hallucination. Specific inputs such as Queen Anne furniture are vital to guiding chat. Overall, chat indeed knows it's antiques and how to talk about them!

MY INPUT: **The most dramatic actions in pro football**

What are the six most dramatic actions in pro football?

ChatGPT output:

In professional football, there are countless dramatic actions that captivate fans worldwide. Here are six of the most notable:

1. **Game-winning Touchdown**: Whether it's a last-second Hail Mary pass or a long run breaking tackles, a game-winning touchdown can create unforgettable moments in football history.
2. **Interception**: When a defensive player intercepts a pass intended for the opposing team, it can swing momentum and lead to dramatic turnarounds in the game.
3. **Quarterback Sack**: A quarterback sack occurs when the defense tackles the quarterback behind the line of scrimmage, often leading to momentum shifts and crucial defensive plays.
4. **Goal-line Stand**: When the defense successfully prevents the offense from scoring despite being close to the end zone, it can be a dramatic display of determination and skill.
5. **Field Goal as Time Expires**: A field goal made as time expires, especially when it's from a long distance, can be a breathtaking moment, determining the outcome of the game and often leading to jubilant celebrations or heartbreaking defeats.
6. **Overtime Victory**: In a tied game, an overtime victory can unfold in numerous dramatic ways, including sudden-death field goals, defensive stops, or long offensive drives culminating in a winning score.

These actions not only determine the outcome of the game but also provide fans with memorable moments that are etched in football history.

Write a comical, humorous story or article about each of the enumerated items about football. Please number them as such. Please write two or three sentences for each item.

ChatGPT output:

1. **Game-winning Touchdown**: In a game reminiscent of a high-stakes soap opera, the underdog team, the Bumbling Buffoons, found themselves trailing by six points with mere seconds left on the clock. In a stroke of pure Hollywood magic, their quarterback, known affectionately as "Clumsy Chuck," stumbled backward, tripped over his own shoelaces, and accidentally launched a pass that ricocheted off a seagull, a hotdog vendor's cart, and finally landed in the outstretched arms of their wide receiver, who waltzed into the end zone for the game-winning touchdown, cueing confetti cannons and a chorus of kazoo fanfare.

2. **Interception**: In a game where chaos reigned supreme, the much-maligned cornerback, "Butterfingers Bob," shocked the world by intercepting not one, but three passes in a single game. Each interception was more improbable than the last, including one where Bob mistook a beach ball for the football, only to miraculously pluck the actual pigskin out of midair as it sailed overhead.

3. **Quarterback Sack**: The quarterback, known around the league as "The Houdini" for his uncanny ability to escape pressure, found himself facing the fearsome defensive line of the "Sack Attackers." In a scene straight out of a slapstick comedy, the defenders chased the slippery quarterback around the field like a pack of Keystone Cops, finally bringing him down with a

perfectly executed triple-decker sandwich sack, complete with extra mustard.

4. **Goal-line Stand**: With victory on the line and the opposing team mere inches from the end zone, the defense of the "Gumshoe Gang" dug in their heels and refused to budge. In a display of sheer determination, they repelled wave after wave of would-be touchdowns, culminating in a spectacular goal-line stand where the entire defensive line joined forces to form a human pyramid, preventing the ball carrier from crossing the goal line while simultaneously balancing a tray of nachos on their heads.

5. **Field Goal as Time Expires**: As the clock ticked down to zero and the game hung in the balance, the fate of the "Misfit Maulers" rested on the shoulders of their beleaguered kicker, "Toe-Tickler Tommy." With a swing of his leg that would make a ballerina jealous, Tommy sent the football soaring through the air, only to watch in horror as it veered wildly off course, knocking the opposing team's mascot off his unicycle and sending a cascade of popcorn raining down on the field. Miraculously, the football ricocheted off the goal post, bounced off a passing blimp advertising hot sauce, and sailed through the uprights for the game-winning field goal, sparking a celebration that could be heard in outer space.

6. **Overtime Victory**: In a heart-stopping overtime showdown that had fans on the edge of their seats, the "Hapless Heroes" and their arch-rivals, the "Bumbling Bandits," battled tooth and nail for supremacy. Just when it seemed like the game would end in a tie, the hero of the hour, "Lucky Larry," scooped up a fumble that had been kicked around like a wayward beach ball, and dashed 99 yards to glory, sealing the victory and cementing his status as the most fortunate man in football history.

My comments:

The first output from chat was rather bland and quite unacceptable. Then I asked chat to try again. The result above was much better. As you have probably observed already, asking chat to list items and then use that same list as the input to a second pass through chat is an efficient and fast way to get a good result. Use chat output to create chat input! I am thrilled with the efficiency boost it gives. The sentence, "... bringing him down with a perfectly executed triple-decker sandwich sack, complete with extra mustard." is completely out of context as it seems to confuse sacking a quarterback with a take-out sack containing a sandwich with extra mustard!

MY INPUT: Family vacation— checking into the hotel

(Note: the previous vacation story was a family staying at a condo.)

Step one, check into the hotel. For some technicality, the hotel wouldn't accept the points I had accumulated on its loyalty program. The pool was under maintenance and not open, so the kids were absolutely heartbroken and started acting out. The room overlooked the dumpster and an ugly parking lot, so we had to change rooms. The new room was next to a noisy ice machine—more frustration. And when we got to yet another room, the maids had overused an obnoxious "sweet" smelling room freshener. One elevator was out of service, so it took twice as long to get to the free breakfast that was out of eggs, cereal, muffins, toast, and coffee! The fitness center stunk as the circulation fan apparently was not working. The luggage cart had one wheel out of whack so as I pushed it down the hallway it kept running into the left wall. Finally, on the upside, the room had a wonderful 65-inch TV that worked along with a remote control that actually worked so the kids were happy. Also, the near-by theme park was open after emergency reconstruction, so between the TV and the theme park, everyone was happy.

ChatGPT output:

Vacation Chronicles: The Comedy of Errors

Ah, the family vacation—the epitome of relaxation, bonding, and, if you're particularly lucky, a comedy of errors that would make even the most seasoned sitcom writer jealous. Join me on a journey through the chaos and calamity of our recent escapade, where every mishap seemed determined to thwart our quest for holiday bliss.

Step one: Check into the hotel. Simple, right? Wrong. As I confidently approached the front desk, armed with my carefully accumulated loyalty points, I was met with a technicality so absurd it could only exist in the twilight zone of vacation nightmares. The hotel, it seemed, had decided to shun my hard-earned points, leaving me staring incredulously at a receptionist who seemed more interested in rearranging paper clips than resolving my plight.

But wait, there's more. The pool, that shimmering oasis of aquatic joy promised in the glossy brochure, was cruelly under maintenance—a fact that shattered the dreams of my pint-sized companions and unleashed a storm of tantrums that would have put Shakespearean drama to shame.

As if that wasn't enough, our initial room boasted a view that could only be described as "dumpster chic," complete with a soundtrack provided by the bustling parking lot below. With heavy hearts and heavier luggage, we embarked on a room-changing odyssey, navigating through a maze of noisy ice machines and overpowering room fresheners until we stumbled upon a sanctuary free from olfactory assault.

But alas, our trials were far from over. A lone elevator, presumably exhausted from its Herculean efforts, had decided to take an indefinite hiatus, forcing us to embark on a stair-climbing expedition that left us gasping for breath and questioning the wisdom of ever leaving home.

And then came breakfast—a beacon of hope in a sea of despair. Or so we thought. Imagine our dismay upon discovering that the free morning feast had been plundered by ravenous early risers, leaving behind a barren wasteland devoid of eggs, cereal, and even the humble muffin. It was a culinary catastrophe of epic proportions, prompting whispered discussions of staging a mutiny in the name of toast and coffee.

But fear not, dear reader, for amidst the chaos and confusion, a glimmer of light emerged. A room adorned with a magnificent 65-inch TV, its radiant glow beckoning us like a siren song of technological delight. And miracle of miracles, a remote control that actually worked—an achievement worthy of celebration in its own right.

And so, with the promise of theme park adventures on the horizon and the comforting glow of the television to guide us, we soldiered on, laughing in the face of adversity and embracing the absurdity of it all. For in the end, isn't that what family vacations are all about? The memories forged in the fires of chaos, the bonds strengthened by shared misadventures, and the knowledge that no matter how many wheels fall off the luggage cart, we'll always have each other.

My comments:

This output was an example of excellent writing. The phrase "dumpster chic" was a hallucination or context error. For this story, chat responded in about three seconds compared to the typical two seconds—possibly because the input was longer and more specific than some of the other inputs. One sequence appears to be in error. I inputted one elevator was out of service, so it took longer to go to breakfast, and it changed it to climbing up to the room. This just proves that chat output needs to be thoroughly proofread. I suspect that chat wanted to focus on the difficulty of climbing upstairs while I was focusing on everybody being hungry and wanting to go downstairs to breakfast.

MY INPUT: **A day at the breach**

Write a lengthy humorous and comical story of the family going to the beach. Include all the preparation including sand toys, bathing suits, umbrellas, and the challenge of fitting all this critical beach gear into the car. Include sandcastles and waves and a child almost getting pulled out into dangerous riptides and mom's highly emotional reaction. Then most importantly, talk about coming back to the car with overly tired children who "accidently" distribute sand all over the seats and the floor and, of course, when they get home the remainder of the sand (quite a bit) finds it way on the bathroom floor, in the tub, and even a bit the bed! Show the parents reaction to sand in the bed!

ChatGPT output:

Ah, a classic family beach day adventure! Let's dive into this comical tale:

Once upon a time in the bustling suburbia of Anywhereville, the Johnson family was gearing up for their much-anticipated beach day. It was a Saturday morning, and the sun was already casting its warm glow, promising a perfect day by the sea. Mr. Johnson was in charge of packing the car, a task that required the precision of a Tetris grandmaster. Mrs. Johnson, the meticulous planner, had laid out everything they needed: beach towels, sand toys, bathing suits, sunscreen, beach umbrellas, a cooler packed with snacks, and even an inflatable unicorn floaty.

"Are we moving to the beach?" Mr. Johnson muttered under his breath as he surveyed the mountain of beach gear.

After an intense round of packing negotiations and strategic adjustments, they finally managed to squeeze everything into the car. The kids, Timmy and Lily, were bouncing with excitement, clutching their favorite sand toys.

The drive to the beach was filled with "Are we there yet?" choruses and the occasional whiff of sunscreen that Timmy had enthusiastically applied to himself, and the seat, and a bit on the window. They finally arrived and managed to find a parking spot, which felt like winning the lottery on a beach day.

Unloading the car was another adventure. The Johnsons looked like a traveling circus with their array of colorful umbrellas, bags, and inflatable toys. They found a nice spot on the sand and set up camp. Mrs. Johnson made sure to plant the umbrellas firmly into the ground, though they had a knack for catching the wind and becoming makeshift kites.

The kids immediately dove into building sandcastles. Lily was determined to build a sand empire complete with a moat, while Timmy was more interested in creating a sand monster that would "attack" Lily's castle. Meanwhile, Mr. Johnson wrestled with the inflatable unicorn, trying to bring it to life without passing out from the exertion. Mrs. Johnson, ever the vigilant lifeguard, kept an eye on the waves, which seemed to be particularly lively that day.

As the kids played, the ocean had other plans. A particularly strong wave decided to make a grand entrance, sweeping Timmy off his feet and pulling him towards the deeper water. Mrs. Johnson's heart nearly exploded as she sprinted towards the water, arms flailing, shouting, "TIMMY!" at a pitch that probably alarmed the seagulls overhead. Mr. Johnson, startled out of his unicorn-inflating battle, rushed in to help. Fortunately, a lifeguard nearby had already taken action and brought a slightly soggy but safe Timmy back to shore.

After the heart-stopping incident, they decided to stick to the shallows and snack on the sandwiches that now had an extra crunch thanks to the omnipresent sand. Despite the excitement, they managed to enjoy the rest of the afternoon, splashing in the shallows and perfecting their sand sculptures.

As the sun began to set, it was time to pack up. The children, now resembling sand-coated doughnuts, were exhausted and mildly grumpy. The journey back to the car was accompanied by a steady trail of sand falling from their bodies and belongings. By the time they reached the car, it looked like a miniature beach had formed on the seats and floor.

The drive home was a mix of sleepy silence and the occasional "I think I have sand in my... everywhere," complaint from the backseat. Mrs. Johnson could feel the gritty evidence of their beach day clinging to her skin and sighed, knowing the cleanup that awaited them.

At home, the kids were marched to the bathroom where a significant amount of sand was ceremoniously deposited on the floor, in the tub, and, thanks to Timmy's energetic shaking, even on the walls. The parents quickly realized that getting the kids cleaned up was akin to attempting to rinse sand off a sandpaper.

Finally, it was bedtime. Exhausted but happy, the Johnsons settled into their beds only to experience the unmistakable sensation of sand. Mr. Johnson groaned, "How is there sand in our bed already?"

Mrs. Johnson, too tired to care, muttered, "It's like glitter. It just... spreads."

And so, the Johnson family drifted off to sleep, dreaming of their next beach adventure, which would surely involve a vacuum cleaner, plastic sheets, and maybe, just maybe, less sand in their beds.

And thus concludes the tale of the Johnsons' beach day – a perfect blend of fun, sun, and enough sand to keep the memories gritty for days to come!

My comments:

This was absolutely excellent and covered the bases and made a compelling story. However, there was one subtle exception and that was a sequence or context error when the family came back to the car. The phrase, "By the time they reached the car, it looked like a miniature beach had formed on the seats and floor". This says the sand or miniature beach was <u>already</u> on the seats and floor when they first arrive at the car. Great writing but with one exception!

MY INPUT: The difficulty of filling a prescription

Tell a humorous story about how difficult it is to fulfill a prescription when the pharmacy has all kinds of delays and problems and the doctor failed to approve the drug due to poor communications within the doctor's office and the pharmacy fails to timely respond back to the patient. All this for the sake of solving an infected toe problem. Be sure to leave the revelation of the infected toe to the end of the story.

ChatGPT output:

In the quaint town of Murphyville, where everything seemed to go awry, there lived a man named Bob, who found himself entangled in a prescription predicament of absurd proportions.

It all began innocently enough when Bob, feeling a bit under the weather, decided to visit his doctor. Little did he know, this seemingly routine appointment would set off a chain of events more convoluted than a cat tangled in yarn.

Upon arriving at the doctor's office, Bob was greeted by a receptionist who seemed to be juggling a dozen tasks at once. After a comical game of phone tag and a round of "Where's Waldo?" with his medical records, Bob finally found himself face-to-face with the doctor.

"I think you've got a case of the common cold," the doctor declared confidently, scribbling something illegible on a prescription pad. "Here, take this and you'll be right as rain in no time."

Eager to rid himself of the sniffles, Bob made his way to the nearest pharmacy, prescription in hand. But alas, fate had other plans. The pharmacy, it seemed, was in the midst of a full-blown prescription pandemonium.

First, there was a line stretching out the door, filled with patrons whose patience was wearing thinner than a sheet of paper. Then, just as Bob reached the counter, the pharmacist's computer decided to throw a tantrum, freezing up like a deer in headlights.

Undeterred, Bob waited patiently—or rather, not so patiently— as minutes turned into hours and the pharmacy's woes showed no signs of abating. Just when he thought he couldn't take it anymore, a glimmer of hope appeared in the form of his prescription being ready for pickup.

But alas, the comedy of errors was far from over. When the pharmacist attempted to fill the prescription, they discovered that the doctor had failed to approve the medication due to—wait for it—poor communication within the doctor's office.

As Bob's frustration reached peak levels, the pharmacist frantically attempted to contact the doctor's office, only to be met with an endless loop of hold music and voicemail greetings. It seemed as though Bob's quest for relief would never end.

But then, just when all hope seemed lost, a revelation emerged that would turn this prescription predicament on its head. As Bob watched in disbelief, the pharmacist finally managed to reach the doctor's office and secure approval for the medication.

And what, you may ask, was this medication that had caused such chaos and confusion? Why, none other than a simple antibiotic for Bob's infected toe, a revelation so ludicrously mundane that it sent waves of laughter rippling through the pharmacy.

And so, dear readers, let Bob's misadventures serve as a cautionary tale: When it comes to navigating the absurdities of the healthcare system, sometimes all you can do is laugh—preferably while wearing shoes to protect your toes.

My comments:

This is a low point in chat's output—it's full of sequence and logical mistakes. It's almost to the point of deleting and totally starting over. Out of nowhere it came up with the common cold as the problem when the real issue was actually an infected toe! Then to make things worse, there was a sequence issue where the pharmacy fulfilled the drug before it was approved. In addition chat talked about a comical game of phone tag when the patient was actually standing in the doctor's office. This whole story is the worst example of chat going off on its own as if it had been drinking too much the night before. Maybe I should call it "hangover AI!" Again this emphasizes the need to proofread with special focus on logic and sequence.

In the grand scheme of things, I could (or should?) have given chat a more focused, crisper and detailed input due to the complex nature of this medical/pharmacy transaction. If I had done this, then chat might have done a better job.

MY INPUT: A list of real estate euphemisms

Please give me a list of real estate euphemisms. Instead of a tiny house, they use words like it's a charming cottage. If the garden and yard is completely overgrown, they'll say the house is in a natural setting. If it's a rundown house, they call it a starter home, or you can put your own touch on it. Please make a list of 15 of these euphemisms.

ChatGPT output

Cozy retreat - Small living space

Quaint abode - Old and possibly outdated house

Vintage charm - Needs renovation or updating

Serene oasis - Quiet neighborhood

Rustic hideaway - Remote location

Unique fixer-upper - Requires significant renovation

Character home - Older property with distinctive features

Tranquil haven - Peaceful surroundings

Affordable gem - Budget-friendly option

Potential investment - Needs improvement but could yield returns

Historic treasure - Old and possibly historic property

Secluded sanctuary - Private location

Urban oasis - City property with green space

Diamond in the rough - Unpolished but promising property

Charming bungalow - Small single-story home

MY INPUT:

Please give me five more euphemisms

ChatGPT output

Certainly, here are five more real estate euphemisms:

Hidden gem - Undiscovered property with potential

Picturesque retreat - Scenic location

Well-loved home - Previously owned with signs of wear and tear

Artistic hideaway - Quirky and unique property

Renovator's dream - Requires extensive renovation but has potential

My comments:

Excellent list. Obviously chat knows about real estate.

MY INPUT: A humorous story using the list of euphemisms

Please write a humorous story with the above 20 euphemisms

ChatGPT output

Once upon a time, nestled in a serene oasis at the edge of a quaint neighborhood, stood a cozy retreat known to locals as "The Rustic Hideaway." It was a vintage charm of a house, boasting a facade that whispered tales of yesteryears and a garden so overgrown it could pass for a natural setting straight out of a fairytale.

The owner, Mr. Smith, proudly advertised it as a unique fixer-upper, a character home with potential investment written all over it. "It's a diamond in the rough," he'd proclaim, as prospective buyers raised their eyebrows at the sight of peeling paint and creaky floorboards.

Despite its well-loved state, Mr. Smith was convinced that his urban oasis was a picturesque retreat waiting to be discovered by the right buyer. "It's a hidden gem," he'd chuckle, as he gave tours to curious souls brave enough to venture into the depths of its artistic hideaway.

One day, a young couple, Emily and John, stumbled upon the listing for "The Charming Bungalow" and decided to take a peek. They marveled at the quaint abode, its cozy interior hinting at stories untold. "It's a tranquil haven," whispered Emily, as she gazed out at the secluded sanctuary of a backyard.

John, ever the realist, saw beyond the charming facade. "This place is a historic treasure," he remarked, eyeing the ancient plumbing with a mix of skepticism and admiration.

But Emily, with stars in her eyes, saw only potential. "It's a renovator's dream," she declared, already envisioning walls knocked down and gardens blooming.

And so, with hearts full of hope and pockets brimming with determination, Emily and John took the plunge, embracing the quirks and quirks of their new home with gusto.

As they settled into their affordable gem, they couldn't help but laugh at the journey that led them to "The Well-Loved Home," where every creak of the floorboards and every patch of peeling paint told a story of resilience, love, and the magic of euphemisms in the world of real estate.

My comments:

As instructed, this story did use a lot of the real estate euphemisms. One thing I was desperately hoping for but was not covered was the real estate agent should have been the person constantly dispensing these euphemisms. I was hoping the agent as well as any printed flyers or online listings would liberally use these euphemisms.

It could have been better if some of the euphemisms were more biting and satirical. For example, a drainage ditch running thru the back of the property with the ditch covered with poison ivy and overgrown with prickly vines fed by regular springtime flooding is called "a charming rural environment".

MY INPUT: The world of self-driving cars

Explain how a self-driving car works to the average non-techie person. Be sure to add comments about the miles of training required, the risks involved to a rider and the autonomous car, the potential applications for a self-driving car, such as a taxi service or package delivery service (For example, drugs from your local pharmacy or food from your local market.). Emphasize the humorous side and the emotional side from a riders point of view. Make it a humorous article adding humor where possible.

ChatGPT output:

Riding Shotgun with R2-D2: A Hilarious Journey into the World of Self-Driving Cars

So, you've heard about these self-driving cars, huh? Buckle up, because we're about to take a wild ride into the future of transportation, where the road is paved with equal parts technology and hilarity.

First things first, let's talk about how these bad boys work. Imagine your car is like a giant robot chauffeur, except instead of being programmed to fetch you a cup of tea, it's programmed to navigate the mean streets of suburbia without crashing into the neighbor's mailbox. It's like having R2-D2 at the wheel, but with a slightly less sassy attitude.

Now, here's where things get really interesting. These self-driving cars don't just magically appear out of thin air ready to hit the road. Oh no, my friend, they undergo miles and miles of training, just like a rookie cop fresh out of the academy. We're talking simulated scenarios, obstacle courses, and probably a few embarrassing mishaps along the way. It's like watching a toddler learn to walk, except with a multi-million-dollar piece of machinery.

But hey, with great training comes great responsibility, right? That's where the risks come in. As a writer, I can't help but envision the potential plot twists of riding shotgun in a self-driving car. Will we encounter a rogue raccoon darting across the road? Will we accidentally drive through a parade of clowns on unicycles? The possibilities are endless, and slightly terrifying.

But fear not, dear reader, because self-driving cars aren't just a recipe for disaster—they're also a glimpse into a brave new world of convenience and hilarity. Picture this: you're craving some late-night munchies, but you're too lazy to put on pants and drive to the nearest taco joint. Enter the self-driving taco truck, delivering deliciousness straight to your doorstep faster than you can say "guacamole."

And let's not forget about the potential applications for package delivery. Need to pick up your prescription from the pharmacy? No problem, just summon a self-driving drone to drop it off on your front porch like a futuristic stork. Craving a hot and greasy pizza? Just sit back, relax, and watch as a self-driving delivery car rolls up to your curb with a cheesy delight in tow.

Now, let's talk emotions. Riding in a self-driving car is like being on a rollercoaster of feelings, from exhilaration to mild panic to sheer delight. One minute you're marveling at the wonders of technology, and the next you're gripping the armrest for dear life as your car navigates a particularly tricky intersection. It's like a high-stakes game of trust fall, except with four wheels and a GPS.

So there you have it, folks! Self-driving cars: the wave of the future, the butt of a few jokes, and the source of endless amusement. Whether you're cruising down the highway or ordering a burrito from the comfort of your couch, one thing's for sure: the future is looking bright, and just a tad bit ridiculous.

My comments:

Did you catch the quick switch from self-driving cars to ". . . summon a self-driving drone to drop it off on your front porch like a futuristic stork"? Chat threw in airborne drones and then went back to self-driving cars. Definitely a context error.

MY INPUT: The art of loading a dishwasher

Write a humorous story about the difficulty of loading a dishwasher. Include such items as trying to get wine glasses not to touch coffee mugs and putting soup bowls in the upper rack so they don't take up most of the rack. Strategically place every item to maximize loading. Place plastic storage containers in the top rack so they might just dry as plastic typically does not dry even in the most expensive dishwashers.

ChatGPT output:

Once upon a time, in a kitchen not too far away, there was a dishwasher named Dishy. Dishy was a high-end, state-of-the-art appliance, but no matter how advanced, it faced a challenge every evening that would baffle even the most seasoned kitchen veterans. The challenge was: How to load the dishwasher without losing your mind?

One evening, Jane decided it was her turn to face the challenge. She rolled up her sleeves, took a deep breath, and began the strategic task of loading Dishy.

First, she started with the wine glasses. These were delicate, long-stemmed, and definitely not meant to fraternize with the coffee mugs. She placed the wine glasses gingerly in the upper rack, ensuring they were far enough apart that even the most spirited jiggle wouldn't cause them to clink together. But as she turned her attention to the coffee mugs, she realized they too needed a prime spot in the upper rack.

"Okay, maybe if I put the wine glasses on the left and the coffee mugs on the right...?" Jane muttered to herself. She carefully placed the mugs in their designated corner, but they immediately leaned towards the wine glasses as if to say, "Hey, we want to party too!"

Jane sighed and adjusted the mugs again, this time with the finesse of a bomb disposal expert. Once the glassware seemed content in their designated spots, she turned her attention to the soup bowls. They were large, unwieldy, and stubbornly took up most of the lower rack. Jane knew that putting them in the upper rack was the only way to ensure she could still fit everything else.

With a bit of maneuvering, she managed to wedge the soup bowls into the upper rack. They jutted out at odd angles, making the top of the dishwasher look like a modern art installation. Jane stepped back to admire her work. It was an odd sight, but it was working.

Next, came the plastic storage containers. Jane knew these were notorious for never drying, even in the most expensive dishwashers. She placed them strategically in the top rack, hoping that maybe this time they would dry. She tried not to be too optimistic, but a little hope never hurt.

Jane then tackled the remaining plates, utensils, and odds and ends with the precision of a master Tetris player. She squeezed in a casserole dish, slid in some baking sheets along the sides, and even managed to find a spot for a stray spatula.

Finally, after what felt like a lifetime, Jane closed the dishwasher door and pressed the start button. She stood there for a moment, basking in the glory of her accomplishment.

"Well, Dishy, let's see how you handle this load," she said with a smirk.

As the dishwasher hummed to life, Jane walked away, feeling victorious. Little did she know, the real test would come when she opened Dishy later to find out if her strategic loading had paid off. But for now, she was content, knowing that she had faced the dishwasher challenge and lived to tell the tale.

And thus, in the quiet of the evening, Jane learned that loading a dishwasher was not just about cleaning dishes. It was a dance of strategy, patience, and a touch of humor.

My comments:

This was the second attempt at the dishwasher story because on the first try, I gave it a rather long and overly detailed (in retrospect) input and the output reflected this more detailed input. I was trying to guide chat to what I wanted it to say by giving it lots of detail. In an absolute surprise to me, when I gave chat a short and more focused input on what I wanted to cover, it gave a more humorous and interesting output. I have been saying the more detailed input, the better the output. This was an absolutely reversal. You might say I gave chat "free reign" after giving it succinct focused guidance and chat did a better job. Who would have known? This was by far the most unusual experiment. I guess the learning from this is you might sometimes try making a short succinct input and compare it to a more detailed input to see which one is better. By succinct, I mean clearly define the topics you absolutely want chat to use. Stepping back and looking at the big picture, this might be framed as a control issue: do you want more control or do you want chat to have more control. A tug of war?

MY INPUT: Ordering take out on an iPhone app

Write a humorous story about what it's like to order dinner using an app on a smartphone. Include the following scenario: First, I had to find the app, then open the app and select the main category: bowls, wraps, salads, combo dinners, low calorie dinners, kids' dinners, sides, desserts, and drinks. For the main category, I rejected the boring premade dinner and was faced with many options for a base which included choices such as rice, beans, or the "green" choice— kale, spinach, and romaine. Then I had to select toppings such as chicken, pork, fish, tofu, hummus and quinoa. Of course, there were special extra cost toppings such as guacamole, and shiitake mushrooms.

After making all my decisions and entering my families' choices as well, I finally pressed the order button. Next, I selected the payment method— credit card and entered the promo code from my last order. Oh no, my daughter now wanted to change her toppings and add a drink and my wife just remembered the chicken was too spicy last time, so she wanted to change to fish. It was just about impossible to go back and change the order. However I gave it a try, but my heart raced, and I started sweating as I had serious visions of having to enter the entire order again!

Finally it was time to hit the checkout button. The app asked for my credit card information, but I couldn't find my wallet! Finally, after looking around for several minutes, I found it under the couch cushions where I sit with my laptop working at home all day. I entered my credit card information and it said, "sorry your credit card is no longer accepted." Whoops, I forgot that visa card had fraud charges on it and was canceled. I entered another credit card and finally the order went through. Whew! This uncomfortable ordering took over a half an hour and then I had to wait for the prep time and the drive time to pick it up. Oh, to top it off, the $25 promo code was rejected— but no reason was given!

ChatGPT output:

Ah, the modern convenience of ordering dinner through a smartphone app—a tale filled with excitement, adventure, and a dash of frustration. Let me tell you about my latest escapade in the digital dining world.

First, I had to find the app. Simple enough, right? Wrong. After scrolling through my phone and discovering apps I didn't even remember downloading, I finally found it tucked between my meditation app (which I swear I'll use someday) and my dog grooming tutorial app (no, I don't have a dog)

With a triumphant tap, I opened the app, greeted by a plethora of dining categories: bowls, wraps, salads, combo dinners, low-calorie dinners, kids' dinners, sides, desserts, and drinks. The choices were dizzying. I briefly considered the premade dinner, but where's the fun in that? I'm a connoisseur, after all. I ventured into creating my masterpiece, starting with the base.

Rice? Beans? Or the mysterious "green" option—kale, spinach, and romaine? I chose the green choice, feeling virtuous and slightly superior. Then came the toppings: chicken, pork, fish, tofu, hummus, and quinoa. My fingers hovered over each option like I was defusing a bomb. Chicken for me, but pork for the wife, fish for the daughter, and tofu for my son (he's going through a phase). And of course, who could resist the allure of extra-cost toppings like guacamole and shiitake mushrooms? Throw them all in!

Pleased with my selections, I proudly pressed the order button. Next up, payment. Credit card selected, promo code from my last order entered. Just as I was about to bask in the glory of my efficiency, my daughter piped up. "Can I change my toppings and add a drink?" Cue internal groan. And then my wife, "Oh, I remember the chicken was too spicy last time. I'll have the fish instead."

Changing the order on the app was like trying to navigate a maze blindfolded. My heart raced, sweat formed on my brow. Would I have to start over? I prayed to the tech gods and cautiously retraced my steps.

Miraculously, I managed to make the changes without erasing the entire order. Victory was mine!

At last, I hit the checkout button. The app asked for my credit card information again. No problem, except my wallet had vanished. A frantic search ensued. After turning the house upside down, I found it under the couch cushions where I work all day. Crisis averted.

Card entered, I was met with a new horror: "Sorry, your credit card is no longer accepted." Ah, yes. That Visa had fraud charges and was canceled. I entered another card, hands trembling. Success! The order went through. I leaned back, exhausted but triumphant. The whole ordeal had taken over half an hour, but the end was in sight.

Then, the final blow. The $25 promo code was rejected without explanation. I stared at the screen, defeated. But what's a digital warrior to do? I accepted my fate and waited for the prep time and drive time to pick up our dinner.

And so, dear reader, ordering dinner via app remains a test of patience, endurance, and the strength of one's will. May your future orders be swift and your promo codes always valid.

My comments:

This was the second attempt at this online ordering scenario. The first attempt focused almost entirely on the type of food and not on the numerous steps required and the frustration of ordering. This second try used extensive and detailed input— reflecting my real-life experience and was significantly better. Chat committed a subtle logical error: the output showed my wife initially ordered pork but later it quoted her as saying the chicken was too spicy, so she changed to fish. The need for critical proof reading cannot be underestimated.

MY INPUT: **The joys of flying**

Create a humorous story about a flight attendant making announcements. Start with something like, "attention passengers there is no smoking in this airplane or in the laboratories. The smoking section is on the wing where today's movie is "Gone with the Wind*. If in the unlikely event that the plane is depressurize, oxygen masks will drop from the ceiling. Put it on your child first or an adult acting like a child". Please dine with us. Tonight's dinner will be a cup of coffee or a glass of water together with a very small cracker. We hope you enjoy the delicious dinner. Please keep your seatbelt fastened because the pilots will be more relaxed if you do. etc. etc.

ChatGPT output: **(combined with my own writing)**

As the plane backed out of the gate, the flight attendant announced, "please switch your electronic devices to airplane mode." Of course, this only applied to young families with children and seniors while businesspeople and texting teenagers don't have to turn them to airplane mode as what they're doing is more important.

Attention passengers, "this is your friendly flight attendant speaking. We hope you're ready for a journey filled with laughter and maybe a few unexpected twists".

"First off, remember there is absolutely no smoking allowed on this airplane, even in the lavatories, but if you must, the smoking section is on the wing, where today's movie is "Gone with the Wind"!

"In the unlikely event that we experience a drop in cabin pressure, oxygen masks will gracefully descend from the ceiling. Remember to secure yours before assisting others, especially if that "other" happens to be your seatmate who's panicking like a two-year-old"!

"The seatbelt sign has been turned off. So, you are free to roam around the cabin. Please don't use the rear restroom on the left as it hasn't been cleaned since last August. The others were recently cleaned—two months ago."

"Now, onto our gourmet dining experience! Tonight's dinner options are as follows: a tantalizing cup of coffee or a refreshing glass of water paired with a single, solitary cracker. Bon appétit! However, if you're hoping for decaf coffee, you're out of luck. All you'll get is a pack of instant coffee and a glass of lukewarm water, accompanied by a splintery little wooden stirring stick."

"We guarantee it's the most upscale cuisine you'll ever experience at 30,000 feet."

"And please, folks, keep those seatbelts fastened tight. Our pilots (and more importantly their lawyers) are a lot more relaxed when they know you're securely strapped in. Besides, turbulence is just nature's way of giving you a little thrill ride between gourmet courses."

At the end of the flight there was an announcement, "Welcome to San Jose International Airport, if you are fortunate, your luggage will be on carousel four, otherwise, please contact lost luggage at either Denver or Tijuana."

Thank you for flying "Nearly Perfect Airlines."

Who knew flying could be this much fun!

My comments:

The first chat output (not shown) included, for some odd reason, ". . .unless you've brought your own barbecue for the wing." Barbecue on an airplane? Chat lost the context. Possibly chat recognized the word "smoking" and "dinner" and came to the wrong conclusion it meant barbecue. A hallucination? Also, I wanted to enhance the initial output by requesting chat try again and add the bit about the decaf experience and the stirring stick. Finally, I could not resist adding several humorous personal enhancements to this story based on my flying experience. In reality, this is a hybrid story, part chat output and part my writing. Rough estimate: 50% chat writing and 50% mine. This illustrates an advantageous use of chat as a writing "buddy" or writing assistant. Note: this is the only hybrid vignette in this book.

[*] The "Gone with the Wind" yarn was based on an actual announcement by a flight attendant of a major airline.

MY INPUT: **Potholes in the street**

Write a humorous article about potholes in the main street. Include not only the depth of the potholes, but also the damage to the tires and to front-end alignment. Include the unexpected consequence of passengers, fingers hitting the wrong keys, sending out strange texts. It's been rumored that spurious major transactions have occurred due to finger slipping texting while running over potholes! It's gotten so bad that driving down the lane is like surfing between major potholes. So no longer do you have to just watch where you're going and watch the lane beside you to see that they're no cars, but you have to steer back-and-forth to make sure that you're missing the potholes. This makes an extremely dangerous situation, of course. Some are even more crazy —they're more like "pot trenches ". We've seen some as long as 10 feet. Now let's turn to how to get this fixed.

Frequently, the roads are in multiple jurisdictions, which complicates the problem no end. For example the city has part control, the state has part control. the county has part control. Can you imagine three major powerful bureaucracies with their own highly coveted budgets. I can't imagine a more delay prone process. And then, of course, eventually years later, when they finally start fill in the potholes, they hire the lowest cost bidder who could care less that the filled potholes are smooth, or whether they're concave or convex. So as soon as the potholes are filled, we've got little bumps where they are convex and little potholes when they are concave. Basically, there's no quality control by the construction companies that fill the potholes. The only blessing is more and more auto insurance companies are coming out with "pothole insurance ". This new insurance offering is the hottest selling insurance product in the last 25 years!!

ChatGPT output:

Potholes: The Bumpy Road to Chaos

Ah, the main street. A bustling artery of any town, pulsating with life, commerce, and, well, potholes. Yes, those nefarious craters that seem to have taken up permanent residence in the heart of our beloved thoroughfare. But fear not, dear readers, for today we embark on a journey through the treacherous terrain of pothole-ridden streets, where the bumps are aplenty, and the frustrations abundant.

Picture this: you're cruising down El Camino, minding your own business, when suddenly, your car lurches violently into the depths of a pothole so deep, it could rival the Mariana Trench. The impact sends shockwaves through your vehicle, rattling your teeth and jostling your precious cargo. And just like that, your tires are left battered and bruised, your front-end alignment thrown into disarray, and your nerves frazzled.

But wait, there's more! As if navigating the pothole minefield wasn't challenging enough, now we must contend with the modern-day menace of texting while driving. With fingers flying across screens at breakneck speeds, it's all too easy for a misplaced keystroke to spell disaster. Rumor has it that some major transactions have been initiated mid-pothole, as wayward digits inadvertently seal deals with a swipe and a tap.

Driving down Main Street has become akin to surfing a turbulent sea, with potholes looming like jagged rocks waiting to wreak havoc on unsuspecting vehicles. No longer can we simply watch where we're going; now we must also swerve and dodge like seasoned rally drivers, praying we emerge unscathed on the other side.

But fear not, for relief may be on the horizon, albeit a distant one. The solution to our pothole plight lies in the labyrinthine corridors of bureaucracy, where multiple jurisdictions vie for control over the crumbling pavement. Picture it: the city, the state, the county, each with its own piece of the pie and its own coveted budget. It's a recipe for delay of epic proportions, a veritable symphony of red tape and bureaucratic bumbling.

And when, at long last, the powers that be begun to address the issue, they do so with all the finesse of a bull in a China shop. Enter the lowest cost bidder, whose sole concern is filling potholes at breakneck speed, quality be damned. The result? A patchwork quilt of uneven pavement, where filled potholes morph into speed bumps and concave craters alike.

But fear not, for amidst the chaos and confusion, a beacon of hope emerges —pothole insurance. Yes, you heard that right. A burgeoning market of insurance products designed to protect against the perils of pothole-ridden roads. It's the hottest new insurance product, and drivers everywhere are clamoring to get in on the action.

So, dear readers, take heart in the knowledge that while our journey down Main Street may be fraught with frustration and peril, there's a light at the end of the tunnel. And who knows? With a little luck, a lot of patience, and perhaps a dash of pothole insurance, we might just survive to tell the tale.

My comments:

Not bad at all. Especially for a three second response. It definitely followed the more detailed input. I wonder what chat would have come up with if the input were simple such as, "write a story about the frustrations of driving on a pothole filled road." I doubt it would have covered the multiple jurisdictions and the pothole insurance. I just had to give a more detailed input because of my intense frustrations with our local potholes.

MY INPUT: An "are we there yet?" trip to summer camp

Write a humorous story about traveling by car with a family of four (one girl and one boy) to their favorite summer camp that has a lake, sports, water skiing, crafts and other activities. Emphasize the constant "are we there yet" questions by both kids multiple times for the whole 250 mile trip.

ChatGPT output:

The Johnson family was embarking on their annual summer adventure to Lakeview Camp. The excitement was palpable as they piled into the car, ready for the 250-mile journey. It was an unspoken tradition that the kids, Emma (age 8) and Jacob (age 6), would begin their relentless questioning even before the car left the driveway.

As Mr. Johnson backed out, Emma's voice piped up, "Are we there yet?" "Not even close," Mr. Johnson replied, with a knowing smile. Minutes later, as the car merged onto the highway, Jacob chimed in, "Are we there yet?" "Not yet, buddy," Mrs. Johnson said, handing him a snack in hopes of diverting his attention. The scenery changed from suburban houses to rolling countryside, but the questions did not abate. "Are we there yet?" Emma asked, now slightly whinier, as they passed a sign reading "Welcome to Nowhere."

"Only 245 miles to go," Mr. Johnson announced cheerfully, as if this was good news. Jacob, determined to outdo his sister, upped the ante. "How about now? Are we there yet now?" "No, Jacob. We are not there yet," Mrs. Johnson replied, suppressing a chuckle.

The next few hours were a blur of "Are we there yet?" questions. They stopped at a gas station, where Mr. Johnson tried to sneak in a few quiet moments while filling up the tank. Emma and Jacob, however, were relentless. "Dad, are we there yet?" they asked in unison, standing by the gas pump.

"Do you see a lake? Do you see a camp? Then no, we're not there yet," Mr. Johnson said, half-seriously. Back on the road, the kids grew more inventive. They began timing their questions to coincide perfectly with each sip of coffee Mr. Johnson took, ensuring that he'd spill a little every time. "Are we there yet?" sip "Oops!" "How about now?" sip "Oops again!"

Mrs. Johnson, ever the peacemaker, suggested playing a game. "Let's count how many cows we see!" "Are we there yet?" Emma responded immediately, her eyes glued to the car window. "No, but look, cows!" Mrs. Johnson said with forced enthusiasm. The game lasted for a grand total of ten cows before the novelty wore off.

Finally, as the sun began to set, the car climbed a hill, and Lakeview Camp came into view. The shimmering lake, the bustling campers, and the colorful cabins looked like a mirage after the endless journey.

"Look, kids! We're almost there!" Mr. Johnson announced. Jacob looked out the window, unimpressed. "Are we there yet?"

"Yes, Jacob," Mrs. Johnson sighed with relief. "We are finally here." As they pulled into the camp's parking lot, Emma unbuckled her seatbelt and leaned forward. "So, when do we leave?" she asked innocently. Mr. Johnson's coffee cup paused halfway to his lips, and he turned to his wife with a look of incredulity. Mrs. Johnson could only laugh. "Not for another week, dear. Not for another week."

My comments:

This was the 2nd try (iteration) on this input because the first one had far too many "are we there yet?" questions which became quite boring. This one was shorter, crisper and had the wonderful surprise at the end ("So, when do we leave?"). I would rate this as one of the 10 best outputs in this book.

Summary of what I learned from using AI (ChatGPT)

This is the most essential section of the whole book and the most vital and educational.

1. <u>Blazingly fast</u>

It's hard to comprehend how fast chat responds. Almost all responses started in two seconds or less. Some I would say started in three seconds. Let me note right away this response time is a rough estimate and not a technical stopwatch approach. I counted "one thousand, two thousand, etc." to determine the time. Hat's off to OpenAI as the fast response time encourages the user!

2. <u>Superb, astounding writing ability</u>

Chat has a stellar writing ability with brilliant phrasing and writing style. I enjoyed the phrase, "a passport stamped with more exotic locales than a travel blogger's dream." In addition, the phrase from the dental story, "She turned it on, and my ears were assaulted by high-frequency sounds that could summon dolphins from miles away" was quite descriptive and a superb sentence.

There are people who get genuinely mad and irate at chat because it does such a first-rate job of writing, and it does it in seconds when it takes them hours or more to do the same! It could be the better the writer the madder they get as they know what it took them to learn to write well.

3. <u>Wide variety of knowledge areas</u>

Chat shines when it hits a knowledge area it knows and struggles when it hits a less familiar area. For example, chat has substantial knowledge about coffee shops, top Broadway shows, dental experiences, football, baseball, various types of doctors, airport security, and TV drug adds. Water polo is an area that chat doesn't seem to know much about. Other less knowledgeable areas include writing humorous and sarcastic comments that highly intelligent high schoolers might make when their teacher is out of the classroom. I tried this high schooler input and chat could not come up with anything of quality and on topic. Chat also didn't know some critical elements about Empire State building construction techniques, the complex prescription process at a pharmacy, and, of course, dumpsters.

All in all, chat has an utterly extraordinary scope of knowledge!

4. <u>Summary of misinformation and hallucinations</u>

A lot has been written about inaccuracies or errors or hallucinations produced by AI. Almost all AI sites have a warning that the information may not be correct. I was surprised by the seemingly large quantities of hallucinations encountered while writing this book. Here are some examples I encountered.

In the story about the flight attendants, chat initially used the term BBQ. As already mentioned in my comments, chat no doubt recognized the word "smoking" and "dinner" and put them together and came up with BBQ which is totally inappropriate for use on an airplane.

The first version of the water polo story (which I did not include) contained a description saying a swimmer was as smooth and graceful as a swan. Nothing could be farther from the truth. Water polo is a rough and tumble sport featuring lots of pushing, shoving, kicking and splashing.

In the story about the self-driving cars, chat, out of nowhere, suddenly introduced aerial drones.

In a story about Antique Roadshow, chat mentioned gold belt buckles. In the Civil War, these large belt buckles were made of brass.

In the Empire State Building story, chat referred to molten rivets. Yes, the rivets are red hot, but they certainly are not liquid or molten. I'd love to see somebody throw a liquid rivet!

One of the most egregious examples of a hallucination is in the story about checking into the hotel for a vacation and rejecting a room because it overlooked the dumpsters and a noisy parking lot. Chat evidentially picked up the word "dumpster" and checked its training data and only found "dumpster chic" so used it to characterize the view out the window. "Dumpster chic" is actually a fashion term for clothes that have been used or possibly even fished out of a dumpster. How different could you actually get—one is objecting to a view out the window and the other is a fashion style!

5. <u>High dependence on input content and clarity</u>

One of the most significant challenges writing this book was making the tradeoff between short and long inputs. You no doubt have observed some chat inputs are quite short like the various doctor's names and medical specialties such as "Dr. Seymore Spots, the ophthalmologist", and others are long such as "Potholes in the Street." If you want to control or guide the output, you frequently need to give chat clear and detailed input.

Input is somewhat like rolling the dice—you might get a bland output full of generalizations or, sometimes, an output that's surprising and quite excellent. However, if you clearly define the input, be precise, be incredibly targeted, you are more likely to get the output you are looking for. Creating the input is truly an art.

6. <u>Context and logic confusion</u>

The output needs to be rigorously proofread with an eagle eye looking for logic, sequence, and context errors. In the middle of the story about navigating web sites, editing was required to move the password paragraph to the beginning from the middle of the story as that's the logical sequence. In the story about the complexities of renting a car, the phrase, "simulated brake handles" does not belong in the sentence about trying to discover how to shift.

As was mentioned in the pharmacy story, out of nowhere chat came up with the common cold as the problem when the real issue was actually an infected toe! Then to make things worse, there was a sequence issue where the pharmacy fulfilled the drug before it was approved. In addition chat talked about a comical game of phone tag when the patient was actually standing in the doctor's office.

In the story about football, the phrase, ". . . perfectly executed triple-decker sandwich sack, complete with extra mustard" was laughingly out of context.

This next one really baffles me. In the story about enduring the frustrating TSA checkpoint at the airport, chat said Dave put on weight, but shouldn't the pants be tighter and not at risk of "escaping" if he put on weight. I guess we should all be happy that at least he had a belt!

7. Output requires powerful review or editing

What more can I say? At any moment chat can throw a linguistic curve ball into the middle of a story where it doesn't belong. Frequently, it can be extremely subtle and difficult to detect on the first reading but at other times, it's obvious. It's almost as if chat likes to play a devious game where it tries to sneak something past the reader that, in point of fact, doesn't belong.

8. Continuous improvement

Over the course of the months creating this book, it seems as if I got better and chat got better. Chat's functionality improved with, for example, an icon that allowed one click to regenerate the story. Also, chat seemed to produce a higher quality output as time went by. I got much better at the elusive art of input writing in the sense of precisely and exactly targeting what I wanted the output to be.

9. <u>Sometimes humorous</u>

"Larry stumbled upon the perfect program—a thrilling action movie followed by a riveting PBS documentary about the history of cheese." This quote was from one version of a chat output about the difficult of navigating TV programs. I especially liked the phrase the "history of cheese".

From the satire of TV commercials from big pharma, chat used this expression, ".... headaches, blurred vision, loss of appetite, increased urge to yell at your children, insomnia, ... ". The "increased urge to yell at your children" was unexpected and funny.

The following phrase from the dental visit vignette definitely brought on a smile, "The liquid tasted like a concoction of old gym socks and battery acid."

Calling Dr. Max Flo, the urologist, "the bladder boss" and the "stream team leader" sure indicated chat almost had a twinkle in its eye to come up with this!

"Chasing love like it was the last piece of chicken at the picnic" was a wonderful phrase chat used in a story that I did not include as it lacked substance.

"With a toolkit packed full of wrenches and screws (and maybe a little WD-40 for good measure), this bone mechanic fearlessly tackles fractures, sprains, and the occasional case of "I slipped on a banana peel." For fun, should I show this sentence to my personal orthopedist?

10. <u>Can be a writing teacher or tutor and a "vocabulary enhancer"</u>

The phrase "learning from example" comes to mind as a primary method of "chat-based" teaching of writing. Keep in mind that chat is also a one-on-one writing tutor. No large class size here! The key concept is to learn from reading volumes of chat generated text and pay close attention to the writing style. Educators may not like this, but copying chat's writing style could be quite useful—copy first and then branch out with your own style.

After creating this book, I will never write the same way again. I will vary the phrases, avoid simple sentence structures, add a little drama, and make sure the sentences "flow".

11. Can be a "writing buddy" or, more formally, a personal writing assistant

As a "writing buddy" you can input ideas to chat, edit the output or modify the output anyway you want. (I recommend copying the chat output and pasting it into Microsoft Word to do the editing.) The only real example in this book of joint writing was the story about the flight attendants and the experience of flying. That vignette was roughly 50% written by chat and 50% by me. I added, among other things, the part about the lost luggage, the "cleanliness" of the lavatories, and the teens and businesspeople not turning off their electronic devices—all based on my actual experiences on various airlines.

The user, in addition to choosing to change, edit, enhance, or delete any amount of chat output to tailor or optimize the story, can also modify the input and try again to hopefully produce a better output and then modify it yet again if needed (iterate on the input). Chat and the user working together (collaborating) can hopefully enhance the ability to create a quality finished product. Truly a "writing buddy"!

12. It's fun to use

As soon as I hit the enter key after creating the input, I was always eager and excited to see what chat would dish up as the output. It's almost like the experience of opening a gift to suddenly discover the output. As an added plus, when using chat on the iPhone, it would vibrate as the output appeared across the screen. This vibration may sound simple, but the effect, combined with the wonder of seeing the new content scroll across the screen, was almost magical.

Speaking of fun, as I dream of a follow-on book, I can imagine topics such as:

Writing a satirical but heart-breaking story about our medical system—wait two months for a critical appointment and then the doc orders an MRI and that takes another two months and finally a follow up appointment (only three weeks this time) is needed to discuss the MRI results and the actions required.

Comparing and contrasting lush tropical islands on the basis of these classic criteria: sunny white sand beaches, excellent snorkeling, superb sailing, beautiful palm trees, five-star resorts, and a fine infrastructure for money laundering.

Exploring the parental frustrations of selecting and scheduling your child's summer camps such as the **traditional camps** featuring swimming, hiking, canoeing, campfires, arts, and crafts, or the **sports camps** focusing on basketball, soccer, baseball or tennis or the **Arts and Performance camps** exploring acting, musical theater, dance, music and visual arts or the **academic and technology camps** exposing your kids to coding, robotics, or creative writing. And then there are the **adventure camps** focusing on rock climbing, kayaking, backpacking or whitewater rafting or the **travel and expedition camps** (let's go to a new country), and, finally, but important, the religious camps. That's all! By the way, all this was for you first child. You have to do it all over again for your second child! Oh, I almost forgot, all this camp scheduling must be closely coordinated with the schedules of your two best friends so the children can be together at camp! Why did you ever want to be a parent?

FINAL THOUGHTS FROM THIS BOOK

Try AI yourself! Explore, sightsee, discover, investigate. Be brave. It's not that difficult. Just download the free app on a smartphone or access it on a laptop and away you go!

*   *   *